Beirut = f̶r̶...
     = t̶h̶...

Powerful book - author's
              personal views

aspects of society around
her
  the society is about to be
  disrupted

universal situations- human
desire to want to be able
to provide for your family
youthful desire to be
rich and famous

self preservation is key.
finding that security

this novel is universal
no matter what time frame
or location
he novel is all about POWER-
hos has it, who wants it, what they
vil war has power in the end will do to get it.

the fisherman - wants comfort,
support, stability.
works really hard as a
fisherman and he is obsessed
with finding the genie bottle.
challanges - feed the family
moral issue about what
they're doing what they
want ex: dynamite
he doesn't have a son to take
his place - his younger son died because of
a fish.
the name of his boat is the magic lantern -
genie
he wants control - it's a power
issue
⚡the fish that choked
his son represents the
mistreatment of fishermen
by large monopolies

BEIRUT '75

BEIRUT '75

A novel by

Ghada Samman

Translated from the Arabic by

Nancy N. Roberts

The University of Arkansas Press
Fayetteville 1995

6th Printing
Beirut: Ghada Samman Publications, 1993

(Original printing, Beirut: Dar Al-Adab, 1975)

99   98   97   96   95   5   4   3   2   1

Designed by Gail Carter

☉ The paper used in this publication meets the mini-
mum requirements of the American National Standard
for Permanence of Paper for Printed Library Materials
Z39.48-1984.

Library of Congress Cataloging-in-Publication Data
Sammān, Ghādah.
   [Bayrūt 75. English]
   Beirut '75 / a novel by Ghada Samman ; translated
from the Arabic by Nancy N. Roberts.
     p.   cm.
   Includes bibliographical references.
   ISBN 1-55728-383-4 (cloth: alk. paper). —
ISBN 1-55728-382-6 (pbk. : alk. paper)
   I. Roberts, Nancy N.   II. Title
PJ7862.A584B3913   1995
892'.736—dc20   95-13545
                                CIP

PREFACE TO THE TRANSLATION

Ghada Samman (b. 1942), who has been referred to as "the most prominent Syrian woman writer of fiction,"[1] began her career as a journalist and writer of fiction and sociopolitical analysis after receiving her M.A. degree in English Literature at the American University of Beirut in the early 1960s. Since that time she has published a number of short-story collections, three novels, and numerous articles and essays. *Beirut '75* (1974), Samman's first full-length novel, has been seen by literary critics as particularly significant for the way in which it heralds the outbreak of Lebanon's civil war in 1975. It was preceded by her short-story collections *Night of Strangers* (1966), *Departure of the Ancient Ports* (1973), *Your Eyes Are My Destiny* (1975), and *Love* (1974). Subsequent writings include her *Incomplete Works* (1978–80), a multivolume collection of travel accounts, book reviews, and social and political analyses; *Beirut Nightmares* (1976), a second novel dealing with Lebanon's civil war; and a number of other, more recent works of both fiction and nonfiction.

The events of *Beirut '75* revolve around five central characters. As the book opens, their paths cross on a taxi ride to Beirut, each of them headed there in search of something which he or she longs for: security, meaning in life, fame, wealth, dignity, recognition, freedom from fear and from tradition-sanctioned practices which are destructive and dehumanizing.

Yasmeena, a young woman from Damascus, seeks release from the stifling atmosphere of the nun's convent where she has taught for the past ten years, and comes to Beirut with a dream of escaping from poverty and a sexually repressive environment. Farah, a young man from a small Syrian village near Damascus, comes fleeing from an authoritarian father and a life of unfulfilling work as a civil servant, hoping to find riches and recognition through a wealthy relative who has "made it" in the glittering city. The third character, Ta'aan, is a young man seeking refuge in Beirut from the tyranny of fear and from the interracial blood feuds which victimize the innocent.

The book's fourth protagonist is Abu'l-Malla, an elderly man long held in bondage to poverty. In spite of this, he has managed for many years to maintain some sense of dignity and self-esteem by virtue of his religious world view and the resulting values which have given meaning to his existence. Finally, however, he succumbs to the temptation to rebel against his lot in life, even at the risk of the clear conscience he has striven so many years to maintain.

The fifth and final protagonist of *Beirut '75* is Abu Mustafa, a fisherman likewise locked into an existence of poverty and deprivation and, like others of his class, kept at the mercy of those who wield greater economic and political power than he. Like Abu'l-Malla, he is sustained for many years by a distinct understanding of the world—in this case, a belief that one day he will be delivered from want and oppression by a genie whose bottle he fishes out of the sea.

But the city to which these characters look for salvation is a place which is itself in need of redemption, for in it they encounter dehumanizing social, economic, and political injustices which simply take different, and sometimes more subtle, forms than what they have witnessed previously.

It bears noting that in keeping with Samman's understanding of the feminist message as a call for comprehensive societal transformation, both men and women are depicted in *Beirut '75* as being victimized by forces either partially or completely beyond their control, including political corruption, class discrimination, economic exploitation, destruction of the natural environment, and oppression. In the present work, Samman places all these concerns in the context of conditions in Lebanon, and specifically in Beirut, immediately before the outbreak of Lebanon's civil war in 1975. In her book entitled *Arab Causes in the Fiction of Ghadah Al-Samman (1961–1975)*, Hanan Awwad notes that:

> The novel may almost be described as prophetic, in that its characterization and setting lay bare the complex roots of

the ongoing strife. It is to be noted that women's issues are not an overriding concern here, but are taken up by Al-Samman only to the extent that they impinge on the condition of society as a whole.[2]

Moreover, despite the overall realism of the novel—since its ultimate subject is the reality of human experience—one will sometimes find the author making sudden leaps back and forth between "reality" and "dream." Besides being a characteristic feature of many of Samman's writings, it serves in this work as a fitting reminder of the chaotic state in which Lebanese society found itself on the eve of its civil war. Similarly, as Ghali Shukri suggests in his book *Ghada Samman without Wings*,[3] the "Beirut" of this novel may be seen not only as "the Lebanese capital, but the capital of the 'world-jungle'" such that the journey leading to it—what Shukri refers to as "the road of regret"—could begin not only in Damascus, but anywhere in the world.[4]

If this is so, then *Beirut '75* offers a message relevant both to the Arab and the non-Arab reader. Deepening our understanding of central issues facing men and women of Arab society may offer insights into problems and questions plaguing Western society as well, for the concerns laid bare in *Beirut '75* are not unique to the experience of modern Arabs, but in one degree or another are reflective of the "human condition" common to present-day societies throughout the world as they are forced to rethink previously unquestioned values and practices and as they search for ways of establishing communal identities which affirm the dignity of all individuals.

1. Mineke Schipper, *Unheard Words* (London, New York: Allison & Busby, 1984), 83.

2. Hanan Ahmad Awwad, *Arab Causes in the Fiction of Ghadah Al-Samman (1961–1975)* (Quebec, Sherbrooke, 1983), 95.

3. Ghali Shukri, *Ghadah Al-Samman bila Ajnihah* ("Ghada Samman without Wings"), (Beirut: Dar Al-Tali`ah wa'l-Tiba`a wa'l-Nashr, 1977).

4. Ibid., 83.

BEIRUT '75

ONE

The sun blazed fiercely and everything on the Damascus street seemed to pant and perspire. Even the buildings and sidewalks seemed to tremble feverishly, shuddering amidst the hot vapors which rose steadily from everything in sight. The sounds of the city, too, seemed sunscorched, suffocating. For a moment Farah imagined that the entire street would swoon: the trees, the cars, the passersby, the vendors, and the man standing in front of a nearby garage calling out hoarsely, "Beirut! Beirut!"

As a pretty young girl passed in front of him, Farah thought he noticed her cheeks flush at the sound of the name "Beirut." Or was it just the heat? Everyone dreams of Beirut, he thought. In that I'm not alone. But I'm going alone to take it by storm!

"Beirut! Beirut!" the man called out, his paunch spilling out over his belt as if it, too, had swooned from the heat. "Beirut! Beirut!" He sang out the name as if he were introducing a dancer to the audience at a cabaret.

An attractive young woman then approached, being seen off by her mother. The latter was veiled, her neediness betrayed by the clothes she wore. Her daughter wore a short dress which revealed a pair of exceedingly fair, plump legs. Good, another passenger, thought Farah to himself. Three more and we're off to Beirut. I can hardly wait a minute longer! He felt his body shudder at the name "Beirut," as if it were the body of a naked woman brushing up against him.

Then suddenly the car was full at last. The back seat was occupied by three veiled women covered in black from head to toe. Farah was seated next to the driver, and on his right sat the young woman, who had planted herself next to the front window. Her mother's teary-eyed farewell seemed only to have aroused her irritation, and she cast impatient glances at the driver, hoping to prod him to get them on their way.

Farah remembered his own mother. How he hated her farewells, accompanied as they always were by words as heavy and sticky as regurgitated milk. Besides, his mother wouldn't really have cried. No, she would only have covered her face with her rough, perpetually soil-stained hands as she always did when she was in pain. Then she would have emitted a faint, tearless moan. He always felt a cloud of pessimism sweep over him when he heard her moan. Perhaps that was why he'd fled without saying good-bye. But the letter of recommendation which his father had written to Nishan, his wealthy relative in Beirut, would surely offer him some help and protection. Might he have lost it? For the twentieth time he felt for it in his pocket. Suddenly he realized that he'd forgotten to bring his alarm clock and to lock his closet. Or had he?

He wasn't sure. It was always this way with him. Sometimes he would be late for work because halfway there, it would occur to him that he hadn't locked his closet. He would go all the way back from Damascus to Douma to lock it, only to discover that he had locked it after all. Besides, why all this worry when he knew full well that it contained nothing worth being concerned about? He really didn't know. It was his closet and that was enough. In any case, it was neither his fault nor the closet's that he wasn't fit to be employed. But in Beirut he could do as he pleased.

Then suddenly he thought in exasperation, damn this hot sun! I'm about to suffocate! And the mademoiselle beside me has closed the window for fear that the wind will mess up her neatly combed hair! Not a breath stirring. Women are so revolting!

Meanwhile, Yasmeena, the young woman seated to his right, was thinking, ah, this sun! How warm and pleasant it is! It makes me all the more eager to get away. And I love the way it stings my face. Adieu, Damascus, adieu!

Departing the city, the taxi headed for the foothills and mountain peaks, leaving behind the towering boulder at the city entrance on which some lover had engraved the words

"Remember me always!" Perhaps the name of that person's sweetheart was Damascus, thought Yasmeena. But she will forget. . . .

As Farah read the phrase etched into the boulder, he was seized again with a kind of sorrow and distress, and a vague feeling of fatigue flowed through his limbs. "Do you mind?" he asked the driver as he reached out to turn the dial on the radio. The driver, whose face betrayed an indefinable sadness, didn't reply.

The voice of the radio announcer reading the news filled the taxi. But not quite. Along with the announcer's voice one could also hear the soft weeping of the three women in the back seat. Thought Yasmeena, perhaps some relative of theirs has died in Beirut, and they're going to his funeral. As for Farah, he wondered, why do they sob so? Do you suppose I'm headed to my death, while these are the soothsayers of fate lamenting my departure as they escort me to my grave? Looking back at them, he tried to make out their faces. But it seemed to him that instead of a face beneath each black veil, there was nothing but a gaping mouth set within a fleshless, skinless skull. Their eyes were nothing but holes out of which their faint wailing came slowly forth, just as dust and moans of distress waft upward out of the mouth of a mine which has collapsed the night before.

As the taxi emerged from the cocoon of verdure surrounding Damascus and entered the vast desert, the city gradually vanished into the distance. Farah and Yasmeena thought simultaneously to themselves, I won't be back until I'm rich and famous!

༄

Wanting to escape the chatter of the radio announcer, Yasmeena reached out to change the radio station again. "Do you mind?" she asked as a dreamy tune came wafting out of the apparatus. The morose-looking taxi driver didn't reply. Listening to the sweet, sentimental music, Yasmeena felt as if she were a forest, and the music a wind rustling through her, shaking her trees and branches, releasing the high-pitched songs of her sparrows and awakening her slumbering adders. Music had always evoked within her a hidden store of mysterious emotions. She imagined herself to be a lover, not in love with anyone in particular, but in a perpetual state of amorous bliss, with a constant readiness to love, to suffer torment, and then to forget without the beloved ever having known of her existence. The cinema had the same effect on her. She would always identify with the heroine, and after the film had ended she would find herself imitating the actress's movements, gestures, and even her hairstyles.

This fellow sitting beside me is quite handsome, Yasmeena thought. But he seems despondent somehow.

At that moment the car took a sudden swerve. Her body pressed up against his, her hip bone touching him at the waist. Farah began to study her more closely. Extremely fair, quite plump, with eyes as black as night, like most Damascene women. Maybe she's a student in Beirut. No, she's older than that. She must be about twenty-five years old. Perhaps she shops for all her clothes in Beirut like most of the bourgeois women of Damascus do. On the other hand, her mother looked quite poor. Who knows? She might be on a search for glory, like me.

The wailing of the women in the back seat grew louder, and suddenly he was afflicted with a feeling of angst and gloom. If I were to return someday with this fair-skinned, chubby woman . . . would I marry her? Perhaps. We could live in my house in Douma. I would keep commuting to work in Damascus day in and day out until I died. She would get fat and reek of cooking oil, curses, and insults. I would be promoted to head of my department, but I'd also be afflicted with tuberculosis from the cold winter commute. I'd suffer from rheumatism, too. We would grow old, our life an endless stream of irritation, mundanity, and screaming children. Nope—no way.

He moved away from her until he was nearly clinging to the driver. No, he didn't want a woman, nor did he want to go back to Douma. He wanted Beirut, and he felt the need to talk about it, too. Attempting to draw the driver into a conversation, Farah began asking him about the weather in Beirut, about its secrets and charms. But he got no reply. The driver was mute, his face somehow reminiscent of that of a hearse driver. How had Farah failed to notice before that this old, decrepit black car bore such a striking resemblance to a hearse? Looking back again at the mourning women who were now taking turns wailing, he felt a tightness in his chest. He decided to try starting a conversation with the "eligible" young woman sitting beside him. She didn't seem particularly interested in him. Instead, her eyes were fixed on the horizon, perhaps in search of Beirut.

She thought to herself, I'm tired of working as a teacher in the convent schools! I'm tired, weary, fed up. . . . The days crawl by, as sluggish as an anesthetized body on an operating-room table, while I do nothing but teach, write poetry, and suffer discontent and anxiety. Beirut is waiting for me with all her glitter, with all the possibilities of freedom, love, and fame that she holds out, and the opportunity to publish my poems in her newspapers. My heart feels like a bird hungry to fly. I'll never look at another nun. Ugh! This fellow sitting beside me has a disturbing presence. He seems like a village bumpkin who can't wait to talk about himself. Handsome, yes, but a boor.

When they reached the Syrian-Lebanese border, Farah became convinced that the driver was indeed mute. Everyone got out to complete the necessary red tape. Yasmeena and Farah returned to the taxi, but the three mourning women didn't reappear. The driver went to look for them. While he was gone, Farah and Yasmeena didn't exchange a word. They were both self-absorbed, engrossed in their own dreams. Besides, she didn't like poor men, and a poor man he obviously was.

When the driver returned, his silence was charged with unspoken curses and insults. He got in and the taxi took off without the now-vanished mourners. Perhaps they melted into the night, thought Farah, just like all supernatural beings do. Yasmeena suggested gleefully, "Maybe they took off in another taxi, newer and fancier than this one!"

The gray dusk began to enfold the plain of Shattoura as the car went speeding along its winding roads with the approaching night. Up the mountain it went, then through the villages of Ra's al-Baydar, Soufar, and Bahamdoun until at last they began to near Beirut. On the mountain tops fires could be seen blazing and glowing in the night, while in the streets of summer resort towns they could hear the explosion of fireworks and the din and clamor of crowds. They were being greeted by an astonishing celebration. Bonfires filled the air with the aroma of burnt firewood, while the mountain peaks in the distance looked as though they, too, were ablaze. Feeling strangely ill at ease, Farah thought suddenly, it's as if I were attending a festival in which a human sacrifice were about to be offered to some evil deity. And who shall it be—me? Yasmeena said in delight, "It's the Feast of the Cross! How beautiful it all is!"

In the abyss of darkness, Beirut glowed and twinkled like the jewels of a sorceress who had gone down to bathe in the sea by night, leaving behind on the shore her precious pearls, multihued, enchanted objects, and chests inlaid with ivory and sandalwood and filled with both disaster and good fortune, magic spells and secrets. "There's Beirut!" Yasmeena exclaimed joyfully. As for Farah, his sense of oppression and dejection seemed only to intensify, and once more he fingered the letter in his pocket.

Silently the driver pulled over to the side of the road to change a tire which had blown out. As they waited, Yasmeena and Farah gazed at the city in the distance, enchanted by the sight like two young children. They got out of the car and walked around nearby while the driver finished changing the tire. In the glare of the heavy night traffic they looked as fragile as the wings of a butterfly before it is consumed by a flame. Farah felt as though he ought to ask the woman her name and introduce himself, but for some reason he couldn't bring himself to speak. Finally he heard himself say, "I'd like to give you my address in Beirut, but I don't know it yet."

"I don't know mine, either," she replied, "but I'll give you my brother's. I'll be staying with him in the beginning." She was certain that he would throw it away within moments of receiving it, just as she would have done with his had he given it to her. Neither of them had the least concern for the other. It was simply that the sight of Beirut had inspired them both with a momentary sense of intimacy. As for Yasmeena, she got a mischievous gleam in her eye whenever she looked at the clusters of lights in the valley below. She thought to herself, I'll become free, free as a butterfly!

∽

After the taxi passed through the mountain village of Aley, it was flagged down by another passenger. Clad in tattered clothing, he looked exhausted and grief-stricken. After he got in, he uttered a loud groan which seemed to come from deep within his being. "Oh—oh my!" Farah sighed in dejected silence, while Yasmeena thought to herself, how disgusting it is for people to advertise their troubles!

But the new passenger, Abu'l-Malla, only resumed his sighing. He needed to release these moans of distress lest his heart burst with sorrow. His ailing heart was what had brought him to his present state, having just been forced to leave his young daughter, his beautiful little one, in a wealthy family's luxurious summer residence in Aley. He had been through a similar experience before, with all its sorrow and pain. But somehow it was different this time. He felt as though his heart had been cut to the quick. Those who knew him had told him that it wasn't like him to grieve so. But, he thought to himself, what do I have left but grief?

The taxi's headlights revealed a figure waving with both hands. The aging black car pulled over. After taking a good look at those inside, the new passenger got on board. Yasmeena thought to herself, he looks terrified. And he was indeed. Trembling, Ta'aan flung himself into his seat. With some relief he thought to himself, well, I got away this time at least. Thank God I managed to escape their watchful eye and they missed when they tried to shoot me. Meanwhile, Abu'l-Malla sighed again, "Oh, oh my!" As for Ta'aan, he felt a need to weep.

When they reached Hazmiyyeh near Beirut, they were joined by the fifth and last passenger, whose clothes reeked of

9

fish. Placing his large, rough hand on the back of the front seat, he hurled his huge body into the rear seat of the taxi. Noticing that one of his fingers was missing while another was a mere half-stump, Yasmeena recoiled in alarm. As she pondered his strained, aging face, Yasmeena thought in naive amazement, I didn't think there would be any misery or old people in Beirut!

Noticing that the young woman was staring at his hand in horror, Abu Mustafa removed it from the front seat and slipped it into his pocket. Gloomily he thought to himself, this money-lender is going to milk me dry. Whenever I leave his house I feel like weeping, and I look so frightening that I strike terror in the hearts of young women.

Abu'l-Malla resumed his agonized groaning, saying to himself, how could I have left you there, little one? How will this old heart of mine find rest tonight?

Ta'aan stared at Abu Mustafa with alarm. Could this man be one of "them"? Might they have seen me get into this taxi, reached Hazmiyyeh before me, and planted one of their agents there? Will a knife suddenly be plunged into my back? Just then he imagined he felt a pinprick in his side. Starting with terror, he looked over at Abu Mustafa. The man looked half asleep or like someone who had died of sheer exhaustion. Suppose he doesn't intend to kill me in the taxi, Ta'aan wondered, but intends to follow me to my hiding place instead?

But the only thing on Abu Mustafa's mind was the moneylender.

❧

None of the five passengers exchanged a word. Yasmeena, Farah, Abu'l-Malla, Abu Mustafa the fisherman, Ta'aan—each of them was immersed in his or her own world of silence. They were like stars that remain alone and isolated even though they rotate in a single orbit. Their eyes were all fixed on the luminous stone jungle extending before them. Yet each of them perceived it with a different eye. Instead of one Beirut, there were five. The driver alone seemed indifferent, impartial as the angel of death.

At the entrance to Beirut between Hazmiyyeh and Furn al-Shubbak, vendors had spread out their merchandise beneath some trees. In the bright city lights Farah could see their wondrous wares: in nylon sacks filled with water there swam tiny colored fish which, when the bags were hung high, looked as though they were swimming in the translucent light.

"How beautiful!" Yasmeena gasped with delight. The passengers in the back seemed not to take any notice of the spectacle. As for Farah, who by now had become even more downcast, all he could think of was that these diaphanous prisons, suspended in the heart of the night, were actually lamps of death. Without knowing why, he found himself repeating Dante's words inscribed on the gate leading into hell, "All ye who enter here, abandon all hope!"

Farah - unde + fish

Yasmeena - turtle Ni Bird

Abu Mustafa - fish - his son

Ta'aan - the man

Abu'l - Malla - the statue

Two

Her body was awakened by the sun, by his touch, by the lapping of the waves, the scent of salt, the swaying of the yacht on the surface of the water, and the effects of the whiskey which she'd never tasted before now. The endless blue sky seemed to overflow with tranquillity and goodwill, as if it were granting its blessing to the moments in which she had first discovered her body, and the sun. What a thrilling, wild feeling had come over her when, for the first time in her life, she lay naked beneath the sun's rays.

In amazement Yasmeena thought to herself, this is the first time I've ever gotten completely undressed anywhere but in the bathroom. And when I put my clothes back on, I was always safely hidden by the thick steam and the dim light. No—I did undress completely once, in the house of a man I knew in Damascus. We closed all the windows, drew all the curtains, turned out all the lights, and locked all the doors. Even then, I could hear voices oozing out of the darkness and bouncing off the walls, warning of the "iniquity" which was about to take place. Mingling with the cries of my mother, the voices seemed to be coming out of my own body, as if I were possessed by them. Their words were like scorpions covering my body, stinging me mercilessly. Their injunctions were like maggots scurrying over me in the darkness, consuming my body and extinguishing my passions. When he touched me, the voices rang out in a chorus of alarm. Perhaps he heard them, too. He was unable to possess me, and I fled from his house. I never saw him again, nor did I repeat the experience. Ah, the sun, the sun . . .

Her lily-white body lay exposed to the sun, the furtive and playful September sun which knows how to sting even from behind a cloud. She allowed it to banish the voices from her bosom, purifying her pores of scorpions and maggots. Here she was, fair and rosy, pure as a jasmine flower in Damascus.

A small turtle crawled slowly before her over the deck of the yacht. It withdrew its body and retreated into the shade of its shell, then gathered its head inside as well, closing its eyes in protest against the sun and the heat. Yasmeena laughed. Poor thing! It can't take off its shell to bask in the sun. Or might it be suffering from seasickness?

A young man had recently taken them on a tour of the Phoenician ruins of Jubayl. Afterward, he had insisted on selling Yasmeena this turtle, with the claim that it was a Phoenician turtle three thousand years old! Later that day, after Nimr had taken her on tours of the Ba'albek ruins, Sidon, and Tripoli, Yasmeena asked the young man, "So, do you serve as tour guide to every girl you fancy?" He replied matter-of-factly, "Of course. It's a Lebanese tradition—the homeland first!"

Nimr turned off the motor of the yacht, setting it loose to wander wherever the waves and winds of chance might carry it. Then he, naked like Yasmeena, took off running across the deck. She liked to think of them as reliving the original creation myth. The yacht was a pearly white shell, the vast sky had never been clearer, and the snows of her twenty-seven years were melting at last, the snows which had descended upon her during her ten long years of nuns' habits and teaching in the convent school.

She could no longer imagine how she'd allowed her body to move about like an automaton all those years without ever coming to see what a wonder it was. She'd only had short-lived, passing adventures in which her body had refused to fully participate. How could she have carried her body about all those years as a burden, a corpse, a mere means of transportation, or a tool to carry chalk with? Now she was discovering it for the first time as a world unto itself, full of delights and pleasures. If she hadn't come to Beirut, she would have remained ignorant all her life of how she was really capable of functioning, how she could tremble with desire and dance madly to the rhythm of a man's caress.

Nimr approached her, the spray of water in his blond hair sparkling in the sun like a thousand miniature lamps. She closed her eyes, retaining the image of his fair-skinned, sun-bronzed body, his firm, lithe body that bespoke a life of wealth and leisure. His muscles weren't overdeveloped like those of a manual laborer, nor were they shrunken like those of the underfed. Rather, they were full and rounded in marvelously streamlined proportions, the fruit of possessing the money and leisure required to engage in regular, moderate exercise. She loved his wealth as much as she despised her poverty. She loved the brashness and insolence with which his miraculously constituted frame broadcast his privileged status to the world. Even his feet betrayed his wealth. They were smooth and soft, free of the protuberances and disfigurements which afflict the feet of the less well-to-do, who are obliged to wear the same shoes year after year until they fall apart, no matter how painful they are or how badly they might deform the feet. The skin on his heels was as soft as a baby's, unmarred by the cracks that appear in the feet of the barefoot and wretched. Everything about his person, clad or unclad, told the story of a life of privilege and ease. Laughing to herself she thought, he isn't poor like me. He was born with a checkbook in his mouth. I was born with an overdue bill in mine!

But ah, what his body could do to her! His body perfumed with expensive suntan oil and with the softness of a life of ease and luxury. She thought, nothing in the world can compare with the intoxicating sweetness of being joined to a beloved man, beneath the sun, in broad daylight, on the high seas where no sound can be heard but that of the lapping of the waves. At such moments her heart was transformed from a monotonously ticking clock into a drum being beaten with wild abandon as naked dancers twirled madly about in a tropical rain forest. She felt as though she had descended to the floor of a warm, storm-tossed sea where multicolored fish danced all around her. The sea's froth was thick and white. She gasped. The waves rose higher. She moaned. Meanwhile, a rigid, firm fish danced upon her thighs like an arrowhead of sunlight.

Then suddenly, she heard the frightful rumble of an explosion. The boat shook from stem to stern, and suddenly she was jarred back into the world of reality. Before she could ask what had happened, the roar of a second explosion filled the air. It seemed to her that Beirut was trembling on the horizon as if it had been struck by an earthquake.

"What happened?" she gasped.

"Nothing," said Nimr indifferently. "It's just Israeli planes breaking the sound barrier like they always do. Bring your breasts closer."

Then came a third explosion. She withdrew herself from him slightly, while the turtle disappeared completely inside its shell.

Irritated, Nimr said, "Look, I told you it wasn't anything. Just Israeli airplanes. Now bring your breasts closer."

"But this is terrible!" she protested.

"It's a routine thing. We've all gotten used to it. They don't do anything really, and they don't do us any harm. They just want to terrorize the fedayeen. That's all. Bring your breasts closer."

Like the turtle, she recoiled. She felt as though a huge, evil bird were soaring overhead, blocking the sunlight and casting its electrified shadow over her.

"They don't hurt us," he repeated.

She remembered how their airplanes had rained death upon Damascus less than a year earlier. She had been among the more fortunate because only the window of their house had shattered, whereas the house next door had burst into flames. She wanted to tell him about it, but somehow she couldn't find her voice.

A fourth explosion rumbled in the distance. Burying her beneath his wealthy, fair-skinned body, he said viciously, "Get your breasts over here."

So she did.

THREE

Farah before amours

He felt utterly lost and alone. It was a Saturday afternoon on Hamra Street, the elite commercial district of Beirut. Leaning up against a marble column outside the Cafe de Paris coffee shop, Farah stood pondering the carnival taking place all about him. The streets were filled with Parisian-looking young women sporting Parisian-looking legs. Never in his entire life had he seen as many bare legs as he'd seen in the past half hour. Young men moved down the sidewalk as if they were dancing. In fact, everyone walked with a dancing rhythm, as if the entire street were moving to the beat of some wild music which was inaudible only to him. The air was heavy with the odor of perspiration mingled with a subtle, hot perfume. Farah stood contemplating all this with a mixture of bewilderment and awe. He sighed, thinking again of how lost and alone he felt. He wondered in dismay if he would ever find Nishan.

Ever since his arrival in Beirut, Farah had been loitering, possessed by a sense of distress and confusion. There was all the filth in the vegetable market, the poverty and misery in the Burj neighborhood and elsewhere, the indifference on Hamra Street, and all the wealth—the luxury cars, the women, the jewelry, the perfumes, and the pampered dogs, in brocaded, embroidered outfits casting haughty glances all about them. Once when he accidentally stepped on a dog's foot, he even found himself saying, "Excuse me, sir!"

Meanwhile, he felt increasingly lost and helpless. Outside the Horseshoe Cafe, people had gathered around a man who was making a small monkey dance. The monkey appeared to be afraid of the crowd, but no less afraid of his master's stick. As for Farah, he was equally fearful of the crowd, the monkey, and the monkey's master. The throngs coming out of a nearby theater, still in a clamorous mood, seemed to have found in the innocent creature an outlet for some of the suppressed bitterness which they hadn't managed to purge themselves of by watching the violent karate and horror films shown in Beirut's ubiquitous movie houses. The crowd's whistling and laughter seemed to bear little connection to the monkey's performance, as if the monkey were merely an excuse for them to give vent to vague, repressed emotions. Then suddenly there resounded an explosion which shook the street and everything in it. But no one evinced the slightest alarm or dismay. Some looked skyward, while others didn't bother, engrossed in the monkey's antics.

"What happened?" Farah asked a one-armed man who was partly beggar, partly Chiclets vendor.

"They're Israeli planes," he replied.

"Are they bombing?"

"I don't know. People say they only make noise."

Two more explosions came in quick succession, but rather than looking up in alarm, the crowd just grew more uproarious in their attempts to get the monkey to dance. Incredulous, Farah thought to himself, here they are breaking the sound barrier as a way of announcing their hostile presence, and no one pays the least attention! As soon as the monkey heard the explosions, it covered its face with its hands and cowered, trembling, on the pavement, refusing to respond to its master's commands. Despite the beating it received, it continued to cover its face as if it didn't want to see what was happening. Then, pressing its face to the pavement and turning its behind to its audience, it began to whimper. At this, everyone burst into raucous laughter. All Farah could do was mutter to himself, "They're mad—they're absolutely mad. . . ."

As he recalled what had happened less than a year earlier in Damascus when the very same airplanes had flown overhead, a feeling of dizziness swept over him and he, like the monkey, buried his face in his hands. As the crowd shouted more loudly, demanding that the monkey dance, the fires of Damascus burned inside Farah's head, dismembered corpses lay strewn about its streets, the stench of burning human flesh filled his nostrils, and the sound of collapsing walls rang in his ears. He stood on the curb, flooded with a bitter sensation which felt like the urge to vomit and to weep at the same time. For the hundredth time, he reached into his pocket and felt for his father's letter to Nishan. It seemed he'd never make contact with him.

Farah thought, here I am loitering in the streets of Beirut with a letter of recommendation in my pocket to this rich relative of mine whom I haven't seen since I was a child. The last time I saw him was when he left to come to Beirut. Then he achieved success and became a model for all the boys in Douma. It won't be hard for me to recognize him, since there's hardly a magazine whose society page he hasn't appeared on: smiling at the camera, talking and waving, dancing with a bare-backed beauty, nonchalantly holding a glass of whiskey. All of his pictures are redolent of sweet perfume and money. Ah, yes, money, not to mention fame, women, glory and . . . and . . . and . . .

But Farah had had no idea how difficult it would be to make contact with a man like Nishan: president of the board of directors of the Ninesko Public Relations Firm, commercial manager of a famous brand of shoes and a new brand of toothpaste, as well as the middleman for a major weapons dealer. And besides selling tanks, he'd been responsible for the production of some successful commercial films and the "creation" of a number of new celebrities. So powerful was his influence in this regard that after a new star had risen to fame the previous year, thanks to the propaganda campaign led by a magazine in which Nishan was a major stockholder, the magazine's art critic had resigned in protest.

Farah thought, I'll call Nishan. I'll put this coin in the pay phone and the call won't go through. I don't think anything's wrong with the phone, but I do think something is wrong with my luck.

Upbraiding himself for his pessimism, he went into the first sandwich shop he came to. The proprietor looked at him contemptuously and refused to let him use the telephone. What is it? he wondered. It seems as though something about my face leads people to persecute me. Something draws me to powerful men who get their kicks out of lording it over me. My father, that tyrannical peasant, seemed to enjoy toying with my destiny. He would throw the books I was so addicted to into the bonfires that he used to set for burning weeds. He'd bellow at me, "Instead of wasting your life thinking and obsessing, you ought to be like Nishan!" If I went out to sing among the trees, he would shout, "That voice of yours could be turned into a fortune. I'm going to turn you over to my cousin Nishan. He'll pour you into the right mold—a golden one!" I myself love gold and riches. After all, riches mean freedom, time, travel, being able to buy books and records, and not being subservient to Adil, director of the National Library where I used to work. Money means beautiful women with soft hands and long, painted fingernails. Money . . . But where is Nishan?

Finally, someone answered the telephone when Farah called. A woman spoke to him in French, and he didn't understand a word. When this happened for the sixth time, he begged her to speak to him in Arabic, and she hung up on him. Cruelty—there was an atmosphere of cruelty that he became aware of whenever he tried to make a move in this strange city. He was constantly hearing the echoes of a long drawn-out wail wherever he went. Ever since the night of his arrival, the mysterious sound of mournful weeping had haunted him. It was as if it had taken up residence in his soul and refused to be dislodged. He was aware of it the way a fine-tuned radar detects the presence of things that can't be perceived by the unaided senses. For some unknown reason, he'd always possessed a special sensitivity to cries of distress, perhaps because he himself had uttered them so often. Or perhaps because he was constantly aware in some vague way that he was a ship bound to sink, just as every human being is, though few are so conscious of it. Money, fame, and women were drugs which he intended to try in an effort to forget the inevitability of his own demise. However uncertain their effects might be, he'd try them even if he had to join in league with Satan himself. But the experience was proving to be more taxing than he had expected. Something about the climate of this city seemed to be slowly poisoning him, as if it were enveloped by a rare, venomous gas. Others had become accustomed to the gas and had decided to live with it. But why all these explanations? Why not just admit that he was obsessed with delusions? The mournful wailing that he had heard in the dawn hours of the day after his arrival in Beirut had filled him with anxiety and distress, causing him to see his entire journey as a portent of approaching calamity.

He was staying at the Honey Hotel on Burj Square. However, there was no honey in it. In fact, there was nothing there but bitterness. It dripped from the filthy, mildewed walls and could be heard in the creaking of the wooden drawer in his ancient bedside table. He could see it in the eyes of the shabby women who floated about like ghosts of some bygone massacre, slipping into the rooms of poor, worn-out men like him. Not to mention the pungent odor of bedbugs which permeated every nook and cranny.

Just as dawn was approaching, Farah was awakened by a piercing cry for help. The scream was high pitched and sharp, and in the first threads of dawn and the silence of the city, it seemed as though the sound must have been heard all over the universe. Farah jumped to the window and tried in vain to open it. It was rusty and old, and he couldn't see anything through the cracks in the half-shattered glass. But the cry grew louder, incessant and piercing like the scream of someone being tortured. It was neither a woman's cry nor a man's. It was simply the cry of a heart in such agony that at one and the same moment it was about to burst and to resign itself to its pain, as if it were the heart of the city itself.

He ran to the sitting room, nearly tripping over the aging, threadbare furniture, then to the balcony. He didn't see anyone or anything, yet he continued to hear the sound. He ran then to wake up one of the hotel employees who, seeing how he was quaking, said to him irritably, "You must be new around here. This type of thing happens all the time. Don't you know that Mutanabbi Street, where the prostitutes work, is on Shuhada' Square right behind our hotel? Besides, I don't hear anything!"

Farah returned to his room and to the stench of bedbugs

in his pillow. He managed to get to sleep, then began to dream. Or was it really a dream? In a semiwakeful state he dreamed of a cross made of rusty water pipes to which he had been tied with rats' tails. All around him fires were blazing. There was a woman laughing nearby, saying, "It's the Feast of the Cross!" And just as he felt he was about to suffocate, he began to fall. Down, down he went, as the neon lights of the cinema cut into him like knife blades. He could see the name of some film written on a long, naked leg. Meanwhile, he continued to choke on the smoke as the hot blaze began to sear his eyes.

Farah awoke in a panic. Fire had broken out in the aging hotel, and screams rang out everywhere. He fled like a madman. But when he managed at last to escape the danger, he stood on the pavement in a daze, indifferent to his safety.

❧

He didn't know how long he had been wandering down Hamra Street and its side alleys. But at one point he came across the monkey grinder asleep on the sidewalk, the monkey nestled in his arms. With a shudder he wondered, what kind of infernal tie binds those who form alliances for the sheer sake of survival, even if one of them happens to be a monkey! He then found himself thinking of Nishan again. He had gone to Nishan's address after giving up on telephone calls and vain attempts to communicate with his French-speaking secretary. It was a huge building, with cars going into a large opening leading inside. Farah waited at the door for several days without even catching a glimpse of Nishan. The doorman refused to let him in and kept a constant eye on him like a suspicious guard dog. Meanwhile, Farah's suitcase remained in his hotel room just as it had been when he arrived. For some reason he hadn't been able to bring himself to open it.

Finally he managed to get past the doorman and slip inside. He spent quite awhile wandering back and forth between four elevators which, unless he came running out at top speed, would close their doors of iron upon him, indifferent to his body of flesh. Finally he read on one of the doors:

Ninesko Public Relations Firm. He was greeted by a receptionist wearing white spectacles who licked her lips nervously after every word.

"Nishan Bey is in Europe," she informed him. "Come back in a few days with the letter. What was the name of the person who wrote your recommendation?"

"My father, Ashour Ashour from Douma."

With barely concealed disgust she replied, "It's a pleasure to meet you."

Her look of disdain continued to haunt him wherever he went. He felt as though all of Beirut looked at him in the same way. The words of the hotel employee rang in his ears like a hammer and anvil, "If you've got a piaster, you're worth a piaster." But his piasters were about to run out. He didn't amount to anything in this rapacious city.

He looked around him. Cars were dashing about like mad, while illumined windows stared at him indifferently from every direction. Hundreds of houses, hundreds of windows, hundreds of faces beyond the windows. He thought about how life must be on the other side, its warmth nearly brushing against his cheek, its intimate murmurs whispering in his ears. Yet he remained utterly alone.

No one paid him the least notice, as if this crowded city had come into existence for no other purpose than to torment the lonely. He decided to go into the first restaurant he came to and devour a tasty meal, even if it cost him his last coin. He had always loved good food, and in this city they had brilliant methods of making it mouthwatering and inviting. True, it would give him indigestion later on, but he couldn't resist.

He went into Popeye's Restaurant, where he had first discovered the wonders of pizza. As he waited impatiently for his food to arrive, he noticed two lovers at a table nearby. As he eyed them from behind his newspaper he thought to himself—like all lonely hearts who frequent restaurants—I'll just pretend to be engrossed in reading the news as I steal glances at the contented and happy!

The two lovers drew their faces close as they spoke, drinking deeply from one another's breath. How sweet the sight of lovers can be, and how cruel! he mused. Never in my life have I sat like that with a woman, sipping wine in a dimly lit restaurant. My hand would touch her thigh under the table; we would shudder in excitement and dream of all the pleasures we would enjoy together.

When the waiter brought the two lovers their orders, they abruptly discontinued their cooing and dove into the food, now ignoring each other. Farah felt a twinge of disappointment but was soon distracted by his own brimming plate. He picked up a bottle of catsup, shook it slightly, and opened it with some difficulty. Then a rare occurrence took place. Its viscous liquid shot out in a semiexplosion, its wet, crimson contents spattering his face, hands, and clothes. After sitting there for a moment in a daze, he was suddenly overcome by a sense of horror from seeing himself covered with what looked like blood. He felt like someone who had just been killed and was still covered with his freshly spilled blood, or like a blood-anointed sacrificial victim. He recalled his arrival in Beirut on the eve of the Feast of the Cross, followed by the unidentified cry of lament which he had heard in the dawn hours of the following morning. Seeing this gory substance all over him, he was filled with a nameless but overwhelming angst. The waiter came running toward him apologetically with a wet rag. However, Farah didn't see him. And without knowing where he was going, he fled from the restaurant to wander aimlessly through the streets.

When he returned to the hotel, he was surprised to find that the goldfish vendor had brought out a new display, the tiny fish for sale swimming about in their water-filled nylon bags. Seen against the glare of the lights shining through the bags from behind, the fish looked suspended in pools of light, traveling in time yet imprisoned forever within these fragile, transparent vessels. Looking at them, Farah was all the more acutely aware of his sorrow and isolation, prisoner of a nameless fate just like these fish.

Engrossed in such thoughts, he paused in front of them for a moment, contemplating them as they darted desperately about, butting their heads against the sides of their translucent prisons. He suddenly noticed that one particular fish had facial features strikingly similar to his own. It was swimming frantically to and fro, its head colliding continuously with the sides of the nylon bag as it searched in vain for an outlet to the sea. But there was none. . . .

Just then he was cornered by someone wanting to sell him a lottery ticket. A lottery ticket for him? What bad luck! But he bought one anyway.

FOUR

When Abu Mustafa the fisherman woke up, it was still pitch dark. Nevertheless, he decided: It's time to go to work. The thieves and I do our work at the same time.

He pulled himself out of his narrow bed and noticed that the stuffing of his pillow had begun hanging out of its threadbare case. He coughed violently and felt as though his joints were too weak to support him. However, when he thought about the magic lamp, he found strength in himself that he hadn't dreamed of. So, filled suddenly with vigor, zeal, and a renewed longing to meet up with it at last, he headed off for the seaside.

The magic lamp!

For thirty years he'd been going out to fish every night, every night without fail. For thirty years he had dreamed that one day the magic lamp would emerge from the sea, having been caught in his net. It would be old and rusty, but he'd recognize it. He would rub it three times, and a genie would rise up in a pillar of smoke, awesome and terrible as the night. Then it would kneel before him and say, "Master! Master! Your wish is my command!" He would make all three of his humble wishes: a clean house, a reasonable income, and the ability to earn enough to meet his children's needs and to pay for treatment for his tubercular lung. He would stare at the genie enviously and ask him who he was. And if he could muster enough courage, he would ask him his name. He would say to him, "Why do you have the ability to accomplish anything you please, but I don't?"

For thirty years Abu Mustafa had been growing more powerless and dwarf-like as life's difficulties beat down upon him. He was withering, becoming more and more insignificant and tiny, like a giant held prisoner within the "bottle" of his body.

But he also dreamed of the giant who lived inside the magic lamp, and this dream alone kept him going. It was his own secret, a secret which he had shared with no one but his son Mustafa. His fishing companions made fun of him for his habit of counting his catch one fish at a time when they brought up the nets. He didn't tell them that he wasn't counting the fish, but rather, was looking for the lamp.

Somewhere in the Awza`i district of Beirut located near the seashore, through dusty, narrow alleyways where the houses smelled of jasmine, incense, and tobacco burning in lit water pipes, Abu Mustafa walked along silently, on his way to the seashore with his eldest son, Mustafa, behind him.

Suddenly the path became narrower, and the area where they were walking grew dark. Abu Mustafa knew the path, having followed it every night for thirty years, and could have walked it with his eyes closed. However, he lit his lantern for the benefit of his son Mustafa, whom he'd heard stumbling. Tonight was the first time he'd accompanied his father out to sea.

A small circle of light fell from the lamp onto the path. Fixing his eyes on the moving spot of light, Mustafa began searching for a firm place to step, and he was overcome by a powerful sense of having been suddenly transported to another world. He moved along silently behind his father, since the path had narrowed, obliging them to walk single file. At last they came to a disintegrating wooden sign on which someone had scribbled "The Nighttime Cafe."

Mustafa noticed that the coffee shop, which had a dirt floor, covered the same area as a medium-sized room and was illuminated with nothing but an oil lamp. In one corner sat a rusty bed frame on which the proprietor was stretched out. There was a clay water pitcher on the room's sole table, which was surrounded by some old chairs. The place was packed with a number of husky men. Their muscular forearms had been burned by the harsh sun and wind, and in the shadowy light of the coffee shop they resembled solid copper branches. The presence of young boys among them caught Mustafa's attention. They were about his age, but the youthful bloom in their faces had been transformed under the pressure of life's grim realities into a kind of mournful, austere vigor that seemed incompatible with their tender years. Some of them greeted his father as they eyed him with friendly curiosity.

Pointing to his son with his maimed hand, Abu Mustafa said proudly and a bit sadly, "This is my son Mustafa. He's been studying in the university. But he's going to leave school and learn my trade because I'm getting worn out. He'll take the place of his brother Ali."

Abu Mustafa let out a choppy, muffled cough, then spat in the darkness. Mustafa thought he saw drops of blood coming out of his father's mouth. No one made any comment. Mustafa noted that there was very little idle chatter among these men. He remembered a conversation between four of his professors that had gone on for two hours! But here, there was no such prattle.

He and his father were then joined by three other men, and together they continued on their way to the shore along a sandy path which was extremely steep and tortuous. When they reached the shore, the men waded into the water several steps, then got into a small rowboat. Mustafa almost bent down to roll up his pant legs so that they wouldn't get wet, but then he noticed that no one else paid any attention to such matters, so he waded into the water like the others and felt a cool sting on his legs.

It's nearly autumn, he thought, and instead of going to school I'll have to enter the wild, untamed world of my father. The autumn of my lifetime is starting even before I've had a chance to enjoy the spring. That's the way it is with us poor folks. We live on the sly, as if by doing so we are committing some sort of crime. We get an education on the sly. We read books on the sly. We write poetry on the sly. And we die the same way.

Mustafa almost commented on the stinging sensation caused by the salt water that had drenched him up to the knees. But the beating of the oars silenced him. It was an exhilarating sound, and it was made even more so by the boat's gradual withdrawal from the shore and from his world, and by the gradual death of that world's sounds and smells, including even the details of its houses and alleyways. This was the first time Mustafa had come out to fish. When he was born, his father had sworn never to take him to sea, not even for an outing. He had vowed to keep him far away from his own miserable fate, preparing him instead for a better life by making certain that he got an education. But now the old man had finally begun to collapse beneath the weight of the accumulated burdens of having to pledge his boat, the Magic Lantern, as security against debts he owed, ten mouths that opened three times a day demanding to be fed, rising costs, the interest demanded by moneylenders, and the grimness and misery of his existence. And on top of all this came illness. His younger son, Ali, had been helping him, but after Ali's tragic death, there remained no one to come to his aid but his eldest son, Mustafa.

Minutes passed, perhaps more, and Mustafa could no longer make out the lantern in the Nighttime Cafe. The sounds of automobile horns and transistor radios mingled with one another, gradually becoming nothing more than a soft, distant murmur which was barely audible over the pounding of the oars. Then one of the men stopped rowing, and when Mustafa looked over at him quizzically, he found that they'd hitched up to a large motorboat. In the flickering light produced by the lantern, he managed with difficulty to read the half-obliterated name written on the side of the larger boat: The Magic Lantern. They got into the motorboat, tied the skiff to it with a rope, started the motor, lifted anchor, and took off for the high seas.

For Mustafa, the unpleasant sound of the motor and the stench of the smoke produced by the fuel oil shattered the sea's calm and marred its awe-inspiring dignity. Jarred out of his world of poetic vision, he was forced to leave behind bays surrounded by coral-red boulders beneath dreamy, turquoise skies. He had flown there on the sounds of the beating of the oars and the sweet, splashing melody that was produced when the water flowed off them. But now he had collided with the reality of the sea, the stern, cruel sea of Beirut, the sea which was, in fact, a minefield, a battleground where a war of survival was being fought between human beings and their fellow creatures.

Thought Mustafa to himself, the time of reading books borrowed from libraries and friends is over. Farewell, days of writing poetry. What's the use of ink in the face of this sea?

He asked his father, "When do we start fishing?"

"We'll cast the nets now," his father replied. "The light of the lantern attracts the fish the way a light bulb attracts moths. Look."

Mustafa came and leaned over the side of the boat. In the light of the lantern he saw scores of small fish happily dancing the dance of death.

"We let down the nets now, but the real fishing doesn't start until after the moon goes down, or even after dawn."

"Why?"

"Because the brightness of the moonlight tends to counter-act the effect of the lantern so that fewer fish come into the nets."

What primitive fishing methods! thought Mustafa. We've got to think of a better way. . . .

And as if his father had sensed what was going through his mind, he went on, saying, "We fish by more than one method—it depends on the season. But all of them are primi-tive, since all our equipment is primitive, too: hooks, traps, and nets, and sometimes dynamite that eats up our fingers. Every-thing is against us—the sea *and* the government!"

Despite his father's woes, Mustafa went back into his poetic mood and decided to write an ode. In it he would say: This moon, though invaded and conquered by explorers, con-tinues to exercise its legendary influence on fish and lovers alike. And here it stands guard in the heart of the night sky, protect-ing the sea's inhabitants from fishermen's snares and artful devices.

But whose side was he on, anyway? The fishermen's or the fish's? He'd forgotten that he was going to be a fisherman, in which case celebrating the fish in love poems or elegies would do him no good. Earning one's daily bread was what really mattered. But no, he thought, I'll think of better things to write once I'm back on land. His only problem was that he'd begun feeling seasick, perhaps on account of the smell of the burning fuel oil.

I'm not fit to be a fisherman, he thought. I'm nothing but a seasick poet. In fact, I'm seasick even when I'm on land.

His father turned off the motor. They would now wait a little over an hour before bringing up the nets for the last time. They were waiting for the setting of the moon, the guardian angel of the fish.

≈

The motor of the Magic Lantern was now silent.

The sounds that had been coming from the Corniche, Beirut's coastal road, also grew still all up and down the shore-line. Beirut had become a distant patch of lights sprinkled on the horizon, and the sky now seemed to have moved closer to the deck of the boat where Mustafa had stretched out on his back.

There were only a few stars in the sky, with the moon at their center.

As far as he was concerned, the moon was still the moon, enchanting and translucent, casting upon the sea a hue whose origins went back to before the beginning of time, a color whose silvery shades were indwelt by the whispers of history and the secrets of the ages.

He thought, my love for the moon didn't decrease when I found out that it wasn't a star made of mercury, silver, ivory, and perfumes, but rather just another ball suspended in space which, like Earth, is devoid of its own light, made of nothing but dust, rocks, and pebbles. Why would my love diminish because of knowing such a thing? My love for Hameeda wouldn't be any less if I were to find out that she had intestinal worms and that inside her beautiful body which I write poetry about every night there seethes a tribe of frightful, ugly crea-tures. Fantasy isn't necessarily the opposite of reality. It's simply the other face of reality.

He found a kind of dizziness coming over him in spite of the fact that the boat wasn't moving. His father said to him, "Get up and help me cast the nets. Moving around and working will help you get over your seasickness."

So he got up. But he'd hardly taken a few steps before he collapsed on top of a pile of nets. He let his face be immersed in them, since it gave him an odd sort of pleasure to inhale the aroma of the salty ropes and let it penetrate deep into his head. Through the nets he could hear the sounds of the thousands of waves which for so long had playfully pulled on them, and his head was filled with the odor of a slimy, rank moistness mixed with the smell of seaweed. Meanwhile, there danced on his face all the fish that had ever performed the dance of death inside these nets, having tried in vain to slip through the narrow openings and return to the sea, to freedom, and to life. In spite of his dizziness and nausea, the sound of the waves was enchanting, captivating, and he went on enjoying the night breeze laden with suggestions, a breeze that aroused vague memories from his days as a young child.

In the face of the secrets of existence, isn't our mental and spiritual vision nothing more than blindness? But, like a radar, doesn't it also tune in sometimes to the obscure, cryptic signals which the cosmos sends our way?

To Mustafa, such messages from the cosmos included the sound of the waves and the wind, the odor of the nets and the taste of their salty corks on his lips, tales stained with the blood of fishermen's severed fingers, and the rents left in the nets by fish fighting heroically for one more moment of life. Together, they sang a song of the struggle to survive, a mournful, timeless, startling ballad full of ferocity, violence, and tenderness.

His father called to him, "Get up and work with us. The dizziness will go away. Come on now, roll up your sleeves!"

However, it was his poetic bent that rolled up its sleeves instead, and again he was seized by the desire to write a poem:

Here I am on the sea of Odysseus and Sindbad, the sea of pirates and myths, the sea of Atlantis and all other enchanted cities buried beneath the ocean's depths with chests full of coral, gold, and pearls, sealed with rusty locks and lying untouched at the bottom of the sea from ages long past,

> The sea of ancient vessels made of papyrus leaves,
> The sea of the Phoenicians,
> The sea of wonder and the desire to bring the unknown to light,
> The sea of Columbus, of the old and new worlds,
> The sea of life and death, of the hidden and the secret,
> The sea of struggle, and of storms that rend sails with their rains, rains that are fate's cascades crashing down over the boats of famished mariners.
> The great sea which we in Beirut have forgotten.

It grieved him that to the people of Beirut the sea had become nothing more than a lifeless painting nailed to the walls of the coffee shops overlooking it. It had become just a blue extension to the black asphalt of the city streets. It had become in people's minds no more than an advertisement for a first-class cruise liner with a swimming pool, a bar, and semi-clad women, or a fish wrapped in a burial shroud and lying in an oven.

We've forgotten it! he lamented. We've forgotten this god of the old world, and along with it we've forgotten its amazing, beautiful creatures. But it's still here just as it always was, silent for all eternity, with a mysterious, obscure language, a mysterious wrath, an ineffable curse and inscrutable symbols.

"What time is it?" one of the fishermen asked him.

It amazed Mustafa that the man should ask him about the time. In fact, it amazed him that anyone would ask him about anything.

I'm outside of place and time, he thought as he lay on top of the fishing nets. I ride these nets as if they were a rocket flying me across the ages, across the ocean, so that I might be able to pick up signals from more than one age, generation, or place and draw nearer to the forgotten truth deep inside me.

Again the voice asked him insistently, "Mustafa! What time is it?"

There is no time here, he replied to himself, no era, nor even a particular planet. The date of this scene might be in prehistory or a thousand years from now. The sea and the sky have always been just as they are now, and thus they shall remain. It's the same song, the same time. . . .

Then suddenly, the timelessness of the scene was shattered by the drone of an airplane approaching from a distance. It was nearing them rapidly and flying lower and lower, while its engines grew louder and its lights became brighter and more visible. Mustafa was forced to come to himself, picking up the trailing coattails of his cosmic dream. "It's almost one o'clock," he said with resignation.

One of the men said, "It's still too early to bring up the nets." Then he got out a hook and sat down to try his luck with it. Another man took off his clothes and said, "I need a dip!" After diving in, he announced that the water was warm, and he swam around near the boat on the same side where the lantern had been hung. As a number of small fish swarmed around the light, Mustafa stared pensively at the man and the fish all around him. What's the difference between them? he wondered. He's just another fish in this vast, timeless sea. The tiny fish swam around and around him. He could see them slipping gracefully through the water near the man's body. He's one of them, thought Mustafa, another fish in the sea of existence.

Then Mustafa heard something resembling a gasp. The other man had caught a fish on his hook. He drew it out of the water, removed the hook from its mouth, and held it in the light of the lantern. Mustafa saw the fish opening its mouth desperately, as if it wanted to say something, like a dying child. As the man threw it into the box where they kept the fish they'd caught, Mustafa heard it gasp, and he plunged into a state of genuine grief, as if he'd witnessed the death of a human being. But it didn't seem that any of the exhausted fishermen had heard or noticed anything.

What a crime! he thought. I'll never work as a fisherman. From the point of view of the sea or of the poet, there's no difference between the death of a fish and the death of a human being. In both cases, a living spirit has been destroyed. I'll never be able to eat fish again. If my mother insists, telling me it's fresh, I'll reply to her, "I think what you mean to say is that since it only died recently, then it's the *crime* that's still fresh!"

And if some rich friend of mine invites me out to a restaurant and forces me to read the kinds of cooked fish on the menu, I'll do it as if I were reading the obituaries or a listing on the crime page of those murdered!

All of a sudden a stick of dynamite went off, and in the light of the fishing lantern Mustafa saw scores of slain fish. They were being gathered up by some men in another boat, which had come so close that it was nearly touching theirs. Abu Mustafa shouted at them, "Using dynamite is forbidden! It kills the young fish, and then we're left without anything to eat the following year!"

An angry voice from the other boat replied, "Forbidden to us and permitted to others—to people with connections, to people who have somebody to cover their backs for them! We want to eat. Our children are hungry, the nets are worn out, and the price of fuel oil for the boats has gone up. Times have changed, Abu Mustafa. . . ."

"You're right," he replied in a tone of resignation.

They then quickly gathered up the dead fish and threw a few of them over to the Magic Lantern as a gift.

Thought Mustafa, from people's point of view, it's only a crime to kill one of our own species. We aren't yet sufficiently advanced either in our human or our cosmic consciousness to see that it's a crime to destroy any living thing. How I long for the Indian and Asian philosophies that forbid the killing of anything, even a mosquito! What this brutal generation of ours needs is the humanitarianism of Ghandi, the vegetarian who overflowed with such love that he sanctified all living creatures in the universe!

Abu Mustafa came over to his speechless, dazed son with a knife and a fish in his hand. With the fish still squirming, he ripped open its belly with a single stroke of the knife. Leaning over the side of the boat, he cleaned it out well with seawater, then placed it on the boat's motor, which was still hot.

"It'll roast quickly," he told Mustafa, "and then I'll feed you some fresh fish the likes of which you've never tasted in your life!"

Mustafa replied testily, "Haven't you've ever grieved over a fish's death and thrown it back into the water when you heard it groaning?"

His father answered, "Your groaning and that of your ten brothers and sisters—that's all I hear."

Mustafa felt both ashamed and miserable. He thought, all the logic of all the beautiful philosophies in the world collapses when confronted with a hungry child's cry. It grieved him to think that some sort of law had made the game of killing virtually inescapable. Kill or be killed. The strong eat the weak, and the strongest alone will survive.

As the father continued cleaning fish and roasting them on the motor, he handed Mustafa a small fish that he had just extracted from the bowels of a larger one.

Matter-of-factly he said, "Look! The fish whose death you grieve over so much had eaten its little sister just a few minutes earlier and hadn't had time to digest her yet. That's life!"

Mustafa remained speechless, and his father studied him with a sense of deep sadness. This boy will never be a fisherman, he thought. He's been corrupted, he's gone "soft." He wants to be a poet! He's half crazy, wallowing in dreams and illusions. But, am I any better, after spending thirty years of my life at sea trying to catch the genie's bottle and his magic lamp? I'm the hunter of illusion. I'm the one who's been trying to fish up the powerful genie whom everything obeys, whose every desire is a command. So if Mustafa is mad, he's inherited his madness from me, the fisherman of the Magic Lantern!

Then the voice of one of the men rang out as he sang a mournful fisherman's ballad: "The lamb prayed to God saying, 'the one who eats me remains hungry, the one who hunts me remains poor, the one who sells me makes no profit, and the fisherman's boat has grown tired and weary!'"

The eyes of all were fixed on the moon, waiting for it to set. Now a golden disk, it had begun its descent toward the horizon, and it had taken on the shape and color of a magical, mythical loaf of bread which everyone had gone sailing after in a race to take it captive.

Mustafa let out a fervent sigh like that of an adolescent lover at sea, while his father once again began to gaze at him sorrowfully, thinking: He'll never become a master fisherman like his brother Ali was. He'll never be able to take his place. I was wrong to force him to leave school and join me in my work. I made the decision hastily, when I was in the taxi on my way back from the house of the moneylender who's been sucking my blood, draining me dry of all I've earned by hard work and the sweat of my brow. That despicable usurer even took my boat, the Magic Lantern, as surety on the loan he gave me. Ever since that day, the interest has been sprouting up out of nowhere like thorns out of the ground. But Mustafa isn't going to help me as I imagined he would. He wasn't made for the sea. Ali was made for the sea just as I was, and he was stronger than Mustafa, in spite of the fact that he was three years younger. Besides that, he hadn't been corrupted by books or writing. But then he was killed by a fish. To this day I still can't believe it. I remember what happened and I nearly lose my mind. We were out fishing at the beginning of this summer, and it was the first time he'd tried his hand with a stick of dynamite. He aimed well, and scores of fish were floating on the surface of the water. He jumped in and began throwing fish into the boat. He was so overjoyed, he grabbed a big fish in each hand, then got hold of a third one between his teeth and starting swimming toward the boat. But the fish in his mouth hadn't died yet. As it flailed about, it slipped down into his throat and he choked to death.

He really did. He died. Just like that, he became the fish's victim rather than the fish becoming his. We carried him home to his mother a lifeless corpse. I tried to tell her that her son had died, but she didn't understand. She was in labor with our last child. Her face was drenched with sweat and contorted with the utmost pain and exertion. She was screaming at the top of her lungs, as if that would help her child come into the world alive, while her entire body writhed and trembled. Meanwhile, I was shouting in her face, "Ali is dead, Umm Mustafa!" At that moment, she seemed unable to comprehend the word "dead." Our new child let forth its first cry, and the midwife picked him up with the umbilical cord still dripping with blood. Then, with the glorious calm born of fatigue, my wife said, "Then let's name him Ali!"

The moon had now become a crimson disk, like a round, blood-stained loaf of bread. As the men began pulling the nets out of the water, their muscular forearms glistened in the light of the fishing lantern, becoming all the more distended and hard. They glistened with the sweat which had begun pouring off them, like human pickaxes digging into the heart of the sea in search of their daily sustenance. As they brought the nets up, the men sang songs which were more like melodious shouts of encouragement than like singing. Mustafa noticed that their chanting also helped them to synchronize their movements so that all twenty forearms would move at the same moment. In vain he sought to overcome his seasickness and get up so he could share in the men's chants and exhausting labor. Instead, he just lay there motionless as a corpse on the edge of the boat, his brain turning over all the while inside the encasement of his skull. And in spite of his seasickness, the fish kept jumping into the nets where they bumped against each other in agitated, restless confusion. He thought, each moves about in his own way, struggling to survive.

At last the men brought the nets up. Their faces, awash with perspiration and the spray of the seawater, were aglow despite their exhaustion, and they clutched the ends of the ropes with lacerated, bleeding fingers. A few minutes later, the pile of fish on the deck of the boat ceased to stir. Mustafa didn't grieve for the fish alone. Rather, he was tormented by the entire game of living. He thought to himself, for man and fish alike, death is the merciless fisherman in whose net both slayer and slain meet the same end.

When Mustafa got into bed that night, his writing hand was stiff, nearly paralyzed, and he passed out in utter exhaustion. When he later woke up hungry, he found nothing to eat in the house but a fish. He ate it, and didn't write a poem.

FIVE

Not far from Abu Mustafa's boat and those of other fishermen moving through the water, a point of light lay motionless on the surface of the water. It wasn't coming from the skiff of some fisherman who had lost his way. Rather, it was the powerful searchlight on the yacht of Nimr Sakeeni, son of Faris Sakeeni, leading merchant and monopoly-holder on the fish market and numerous other markets as well.

Yasmeena hadn't slept that night. She was still sipping whiskey and roaming naked over the deck of the yacht. She enjoyed taking off all her clothes and moving about the cabin and the rest of the boat in a state of nakedness. It filled her with a delicious sense of freedom. In the beginning Nimr had been quite taken by this habit of hers. He would gaze at her fair-skinned, voluptuous body as it moved back and forth among velvet feather pillows. Then he'd bend down to put on a phonograph record and carry her straight to bed. Sometimes they would collapse together onto the luxuriant shag carpet before they'd reached their destination. As she was remembering all these things with a sigh, she heard a voice say to her with a kind of affected, cool tenderness, "Put on your clothes. Now that fall has arrived, it gets cold at night."

For the first time she actually felt naked. She came in, wrapped a silk kimono around her body, then went back out to the deck of the yacht to gaze at the illuminated fishing boats. Then she burst into muffled tears.

For days she had felt the need to cry, but she would freeze up. Something had been broken between her and Nimr. A coldness had begun to envelop their relationship, and a thread of death had stolen into all their interactions. A layer of rust had begun to grow on their bodies and lips, and his kisses had come to taste like rust in her mouth. What had happened? She didn't know. She was still passionately attached to him, but she knew with a female's infallible intuition that something had come to an end. She couldn't discuss the matter with him, since for the most part, he was still treating her the way he always had. He continued to shower her with money, lavish his body on her in bed, and give her freely of his time and presence. Nor could she speak to him about the small details, like the whispered morning telephone call in which he'd made an appointment to meet someone the following evening at nine o'clock. After all, she had supposedly been in the bathroom at the time, not eavesdropping behind the door. Nor could she ask him about what that childish woman in the restaurant had meant when she said to him, "Congratulations!" and then shot Yasmeena a contemptuous look that only a woman would know how to interpret.

And even if she'd been honest with him about her fears and suspicions, or if she'd said, "I feel as though you no longer love me the way you used to," he would have replied, "The fact that you doubt my love means that your own love has grown cold. Suspicion means a lack of trust, and a lack of trust shows a lack of love. Those who haven't thought of being unfaithful don't suspect those they love of doing so." That's what he had said the day before. In so doing he had removed her from behind the prosecutor's podium and placed her on the witness stand. It was a smooth reply, but unconvincing. Words. Words. He'd sworn his faithfulness to her, but she didn't dare tell him that his words hadn't rung true in her heart, and that the woman in love has a strange, frightening sense by which she can sniff out the presence of a rival.

She thought to herself, I still love him. I love what his naked body can do to me. I feel grateful to him because he transformed me from an icy tundra into a minefield. Whenever we have an argument, I can't help but try to placate him. I've become an addict, and his body is my opium. He likes to dress me up in expensive clothes, then take me out to fancy restaurants so that his friends can see us. I know he likes to show me off in the Cafe du Roi, the Panache, and Beirut's other high-class restaurants and bars. He also likes to humiliate me as evidence of his manly "charm." I know that every now and then he neglects me while he goes out to "conquer" another woman that he can parade in front of his friends, if even for just one night. And then he comes back to me.

He always comes back to me because no one else loves him the way I do and because there isn't another woman in the world who laps up his nectar as hungrily as I do. To him I'm nothing but a conquest; whereas for me, he's been the beginning of a whole new life. When he spoke to me one day of his engagement to Naila Salmouni, daughter of Fadhil Salmouni, his father's political rival, I thought he was kidding. I considered it an amusing joke that marriages in this peculiar city should be contracted on the basis of political interests or business deals between different clans. I couldn't imagine that a marriage would be arranged between two people who had never met before when there was another woman melting amorously in the groom's arms and when, just perhaps, he loved her in return without noticing it! I still love him, and my overwhelming passion for his body has always prevented me from seeing him clearly. That is, until last night. Last night I think I saw his true face for a second.

We began the day in the port town of Jounieh, then went up on the "telepherique," or cable-railway, to Harisa. I wished we would go into the church on the mountaintop and get married right there and then. But as usual, we continued our journey straight to bed without such formalities.

Then a little before midnight he told me that I drained him of all his energy, that he was tired and bored. As for me, I was hungrier for his body than ever before. I told him so, and he advised me to look for another man. I thought he was joking. I said to him, "But I love you. That's why I delight in you the way I do. No other man could give me such pleasure."

He shouted back, "Your body is possessed by demons! Any man would give you pleasure! Go and give it a try! I even doubt whether you were a virgin when we started out. You've played some kind of trick on me!"

I began to cry, and he shut me up with a kiss. Then we went to the casino so he could gamble for a while, the way he does whenever he's in an angry mood. Or might he have deliberately created an argument out of nothing, knowing that he had an appointment to keep at the casino and not wanting me to go with him? After we arrived, we were approached by some VIP, who greeted Nimr and introduced him to his daughter. She was an ordinary-looking girl who wore extraordinary jewelry. And when I heard her name—Miss Naila Salmouni, daughter of Fadhil Bey Salmouni, a member of the Lebanese parliament—I froze. So, this was the one—the daughter of one of his political opponents and the proposed fiancée. I noticed that he introduced me to her by a false name. Instead of telling her that my name was Yasmeena, he introduced me as "Mademoiselle Ibrahim, a former classmate of mine at the university." Then I understood why he'd wanted to go to the casino without me.

Now that his body had been planted inside of mine, might he actually snatch it from me and go far away? I had burned all my bridges behind me. I wasn't even employed anymore. True, he was spending lavishly on me, just as I was spending lavishly on my brother, who for his part was turning a blind eye to what was going on out of deference to the money that I kept him supplied with. But . . . he . . . his body . . . I'd become accustomed to it, addicted to it. I'd been smitten by it like someone who's been stricken with an illness. For all of twenty-seven years I'd been forbidden to partake of this amazing pleasure, and here I was now, ill on account of it, a deviant who had devoted herself to the bed. In my blood ran the passionate desires of all the Arab women who had been held prisoners for more than a thousand years. It was no longer possible for me to experience sex as merely one part of my life. Instead, I'd been vanquished in my encounter with it, and it had become my entire existence.

During the few nights that I spent in my brother's house, far from Nimr's fair-skinned body, I would get the shakes like an addict deprived of her fix, and I would lose all capacity to think or act rationally. I could see my madness and my error. I could even see clearly how to escape from the predicament

I'd gotten myself into, yet I wasn't able to actually do it. When the purveyors of tradition confined me within a female's "proper" role, as a genie is held captive inside its bottle, they forgot that in doing so, they were stripping me of my powers of resistance.

So, here I am surrendering to the river of fire which is sweeping me away, a river of sighs and moans so hot that they can sear and cauterize. Here I am frightening him with my ravenous desire. He can't understand that it isn't because I'm a whore, but simply because my hunger for his body is more than a thousand years old.

I can smell the fragrance of autumn in the air. The wind has begun to blow cold. Is it possible that my summer has ended forever?

Yasmeena remained standing on the deck of the yacht for a long time without him coming after her. She took off her robe and stood there weeping in the night, naked and alone. For the first time she envied her turtle curled up inside its shell. She thought, why don't I have a shell that I can take refuge in? I'm alone, fragile, and unprotected against Nimr's blows as long as I'm addicted to him this way.

Behind the string of lights formed by the fishing boats, the lights of Beirut appeared dim and shaky in the distance, like a red-hot coal that's begun to go out. She leaned over the edge of the yacht and read her name written on the side: Yasmeena.

Tomorrow he'll repaint it, she thought to herself. Some worker will come and paint over my name, then in its place they'll put someone else's, Naila's, perhaps.

But she couldn't really believe that such a thing was possible. She was like Nimr's wife. She loved him, was faithful to him, lived with him, gave him pleasure, and withheld nothing from him. She didn't want anyone else in the world. She was a virgin on the day he first made love to her, and she had never known any other man. So why didn't he marry her instead of someone else? She decided to ask him the next day.

❧

At nine o'clock the following evening, Nimr Sakeeni was accompanying his father on a family visit to the house of Fadhil Salmouni to ask for the hand of his daughter, Miss Naila. He'd only seen her once before—in the casino with her father, Fadhil Bey. Nevertheless, Nimr's father stood to benefit a great deal in future elections from a marital alliance with the family of his traditional political opponent.

At that same hour, Yasmeena was pacing around Nimr's luxurious flat and wondering sadly, where is he? Who might he be bestowing his sweet presence on now? Who are his eyes twinkling for this time? Meanwhile, her turtle was roaming around with its head hung lower than usual. It even seemed to be walking more slowly, as if its shoulders were weighed down with sorrow. As Yasmeena stood in front of the mirror, an inscrutable anxiety and distress came over her soul. She remembered that she hadn't laughed a single time for more than a week. She tried to recall how she used to laugh before knowing Nimr, but couldn't. She looked into the mirror to see if she could laugh that way again, but found to her horror that tears covered her face instead. She decided to seek refuge in her papers and write a poem as she'd always done before whenever she felt sad. But she was unable to. She'd even forgotten about the desire she'd once had to meet with literary critics, reporters, and publishers. She'd forgotten everything. Nimr had become her entire universe, the ground beneath her feet, and now he was withdrawing and leaving her to fall alone through space.

She looked over at the turtle in hopes that it would keep her company, but she found that it had withdrawn inside its shell. The whole world was turning away from her, leaving her alone like an empty shell abandoned by the waves on some forgotten beach in Beirut.

Six

Nishan!

Farah couldn't believe that at last he had met him face to face. True, Nishan hadn't welcomed him with open arms as he'd imagined that he might. He hadn't embraced him with tears in his eyes, asking about his father and everyone in the village of Douma one by one. But he'd at least shaken his hand and asked him to have a seat while he finished a telephone conversation. He'd been waiting now for two and a half hours, during which time Nishan went from one telephone to another, and one call to another. There were secretaries coming in and going out, men carrying thick cigars, and others who, like him, had flustered, needy looks on their faces.

Nishan had flown into a rage while he was talking on the telephone. He looked uglier and older than he had in his pictures. Not only that, but his manner of expression was harsher and more uncouth. Still, the luxuriousness of the place made Farah feel small and insignificant. Both the floor and the walls of the office were covered with something resembling velvet, which made the entire room seem like a velvet-lined box. In front of where Nishan was sitting was a table made of translucent glass above which hung various ceiling lamps, while behind him there was a panel of buttons which opened and closed doors and cabinets.

Farah felt as though he had stepped into a world which was both beautiful and savage, or as though he had been caught between the jaws of a people-eating plant with shiny, metallic teeth. Nevertheless, he settled into his chair. He was utterly exhausted, as if Beirut had brainwashed him, torturing him for an entire month with homesickness, loneliness, and deprivation. It made him feel dwarfed inside, as insignificant and neglected as a cockroach, half of whose body has been crushed under someone's shoe. He could hear a voice inside him urging him to flee, to go back to his village, his books, and his empty, locked closet. But he imagined that its lock had been removed, that the wind had blown its double doors off and then, with a villainous, scornful huff and puff, had made its way inside.

Farah thought to himself, he's forgotten me sitting on this chair. He's completely forgotten me. As far as he's concerned, there's no difference between me and the rubber plant that decorates this place, or the potted flowers or the doormat.

Then Nishan's conversation over the telephone turned into angry shouting. Farah didn't want to listen, but the angry voice forced its way into his consciousness. Nishan was trembling as he screamed, "I'm the one who made you, and I'm the one who can destroy you! Did you really think you'd become a star? I could replace you with a new face at any moment. There's always someone in my office who could take your place. My daughter will break her engagement to you, too. Yes, that's right. I own her, and I own you as well. Don't believe the newspaper critics who write articles about your talent after I invite them to dinner. Both you and I know that you don't have any. As for me, though, I'm plenty talented in my work, and that's why I'll be the one to destroy you. You'll see!"

He hung up the phone and turned toward Farah. He stared at him as if he were seeing him for the first time. Farah felt as though his clothes were shabby, and he could feel his toe tensing up inside his shoe where there was a hole in his sock.

Nishan studied Farah for a long time, then said to him in a tone so peremptory it might as well have been destiny itself speaking, "So then, you want money and fame. Your father says in his letter that you have a nice voice."

". . ."

"Do you know what it costs to become famous?"

". . ."

"Are you prepared to pay the price? The price is, first of all, obedience—absolute obedience to me. . . ."

There was something vicious and hard in Nishan's voice, like the crack of the trainer's whip on the bodies of circus animals. Without knowing why, Farah was reminded of the story of the man who signed a pact in blood with Satan, in which he agreed to give his soul to the devil if the latter would fulfill all his desires. What was that man's name? Maybe it was Farah—or was it Faust?

Farah went back to the Honey Hotel to gather up his few personal belongings and his shabby clothes in preparation for moving to the hotel where Nishan had reserved a room for him. He stared at his things, which were so few and in such poor condition, then he packed them into his suitcase and left the hotel without taking any of them with him. When he reached the main entrance to the hotel, he was accosted by the goldfish vendor with his peculiar wares. As usual, Farah stood mesmerized in front of the colored fish, gazing at them as they swam around inside the clear nylon bags, futilely bumping up against the walls of the bags with their heads. Then suddenly one of the bags burst, sending its contents splattering onto the pavement.

Exposed to the air, the fish that had fallen onto the sidewalk squirmed and jumped around in their struggle to remain alive. They kept slipping through the fingers of the vendor, who was trying in vain to grab hold of them and deposit them in another bag. When he saw it, Farah's heart was filled with such sorrow and distress that he broke into silent, tearless sobs.

Fish

46

SEVEN

Fadhil Salmouni came out the door of his mansion in Beirut's aristocratic Yerza district, causing an unusual stir in the garden outside. The driver ran immediately to bring the Cadillac from the garage, while a number of people with particular needs hovered around the bey, who was a man of power and influence. However, his escorts stuck close to him, shooing away the people who at one time had elected him to represent them in the parliament. They managed to drive all of the spectators away except for a frail, elderly man who was shouting in an extremely loud voice that seemed incommensurate with the slightness of his frame, "I told you that the Israelis had burned my crops and blown up my house! Come and live with us on your land and see what's happening!"

His voice was so loud, it seemed as though he were nothing but a huge larynx.

With the calm, authoritative, indisputable tone of one pronouncing a divine decree, the bey replied, "Time and time again I've advised you and other people in your village not to harbor saboteurs, but you didn't heed my words. You call them 'fedayeen' or fighters willing to sacrifice their lives for their homeland. But they're the ones who've brought ruin on the village! As God said to the prophet Muhammad in the Holy Qur'an, 'Say, work, and God shall see what you do, as well as His apostles and the believers.'"

The old man shouted back, "So you quote God's words to justify yourself? Woe to you! Your destruction is coming from . . . !"

He didn't finish his sentence, however, because a blow

came down on his face that was likely to shut him up for some time to come, or perhaps only until another outburst in the not-so-distant future.

Then the honorable parliamentarian, Fadhil Bey Salmouni, said to his chauffeur, "I won't be going in the Cadillac this time. Bring the small car."

The chauffeur smiled knowingly, since this meant that the bey would be going to his secret flat. So he brought a small Fiat, which the bey got into, gesturing to his bodyguards not to accompany him. One of them took a small revolver out of his pocket and gave it to the bey in case his precious life should be placed in any danger.

The car then took off with him and headed for the White Sands district along the coast. At first the bey was distracted and preoccupied, but he soon came out of his reverie and said to his driver, "No. We're not going there now. Take me to Faiza's house instead."

"There" was where he had his lovely little apartment, which now contained a new little butterfly, one of those fair-skinned tourists. He preferred foreigners, since with them, the agreed-upon arrangement was more clear-cut, and as a result, he could disentangle himself more easily and without complications or long, drawn-out endings. True, his Arab women friends were more passionate and sincere, but they were also stupid enough to actually fall in love with the man they were living with. Consequently, over time they would go from being a pleasure to being a problem, and he didn't have time for problems. Foreign women had a better understanding of life—one service in exchange for another. Besides, they weren't shocked when they found out about his particular needs and preferences, whereas Arab women considered them perversions.

The car stopped in front of the house of the fortuneteller, Faiza. The driver got out quickly to inform her of the bey's arrival. Within a couple of minutes he was in a small room which contained little furniture and was completely devoid of windows, as if the spirits and jinn didn't like such things. Or perhaps it was to leave more room for her to work when a procession of visitors arrived and the atmosphere became charged with feverish heat, tension, and ghostly shudders.

"All is well, I hope?" she said.

"I've come to ask you about something very important."

"Fine," she replied, "bring the matter to mind now and keep it before you."

"All right."

As she looked at him with her penetrating eyes, he lowered his glance in respectful acknowledgment of her occult powers and the presence of her unseen, secret companions. Concentrating his gaze on the back of the chair, which was torn in places, he stuck his finger into one of the holes and began widening it with a nervous motion. Meanwhile, she picked up a pen and on a piece of paper drew some lines and words, even though, being illiterate, she could neither read nor write.

"Exactly," he said. "My daughter Naila . . ."

She continued drawing the lines, and he said, ". . . and Nimr Sakeeni. What do you think? Should plans for their marriage proceed?"

She closed her eyes and a shudder went through her body. The spirit of knowledge that had passed into her body caused her hand to run over the paper and write in human languages. Then it came over her again and she began to tremble violently. Out of her throat came a voice that sounded only partially human, like that of a man wrapped tightly inside a burial shroud. And she said, "I see much grief, and I see blood—a great deal of blood."

Then she started to gasp and shudder, witnessing in her mind's eye a future massacre.

After becoming calm for a few minutes, she opened her eyes, which were now completely tranquil, with no effects of the weeping and trembling of a few minutes earlier. Rather, it was as if someone else had inhabited her body for a moment and then departed.

Then the bey said to her in a tone of supplication, "There's one more thing that I wanted to consult you about. Will the marriage take place?"

She replied, "You must keep this to yourself!"

She closed her eyes again and allowed a mysterious presence to transmit its electricity-like impulses to her. Then, letting the pen carry her hand along, she wrote, "Yes."

He rubbed his hands together, then took out some large bills and handed them to her. Finally, he leaned down to kiss her hand reverently, then rushed out.

After he'd left, Faiza laughed out loud as she counted up the incredible haul she'd made.

EIGHT

The thunder rolled like a cry of terror whose source was hidden, shrouded in mystery.

When the clap of thunder sounded, Yasmeena was alone. The world seemed defiant and full of ill will, and she felt tiny and insignificant against the vast night sky, forgotten like a half-crushed ant. His name leapt immediately to her throat: Nimr. Nimr.

She thought, who would have believed that love in this city would be stillborn? Who would have believed that his fingers, which used to burn with passion whenever they touched me, would become as dispassionate and self-controlled as those of someone writing a business report?

She wasn't the kind of woman to give up. But what good would it do her to try casting the other woman out of his life if he himself no longer cared?

Why don't I come to my senses? Why don't I go back to Damascus? Why not go back before the police arrest me on charges of prostitution or unlawful cohabitation?

Full of trepidation, she began reading the crime pages of the newspaper. Whenever she saw a headline saying "Apartment Raided" or the like, she would read the whole article, her heart fluttering for fear that her name would be mentioned.

The thunder rolled again, and his name leapt back to her throat. Nimr. . . . I wonder where he is now? she thought. And who is he with? Whom might he be gracing with his winsome, fair-skinned, radiant presence?

She knew that she would never go back to Damascus. Not a single drop of water in the river can ever return to its source. What's been has been, and that's that. She had now launched out onto the river of no return, the river of blood.

She turned up the volume on the television in hopes of drowning out the sounds of the rain and thunder. She decided to concentrate her attention on the face of the young man singing on the screen. He had such a masculine, plaintive voice—she knew him from somewhere. She'd seen that face before. She was sure of it. But where? Where, where, where? Ah—she couldn't remember anymore. But she had definitely seen him, of that she was certain.

I've lost everything, she thought, even my memory! Then the program host announced the name of the "singer of manliness" as "Farah." Farah . . . She felt as though she'd heard his name before.

It was now nearly eleven o'clock, the time when Nimr normally got home at night, and her heart was pounding like that of a bird that's just been shot. Where might he have gone? His story about having company meetings every evening hadn't convinced her, especially in view of the fact that he refused to let her contact him by telephone, his excuse being that he was going to take the phone off the hook so he could devote himself completely to work. If he had at least given her the option of calling him, she wouldn't have felt the need to, since she would have been reassured that he really was there at the office. Instead, she spent the three hours that he was gone in agony. Was he spending every evening at Naila's house, like any gentlemanly suitor would do? But he denied the rumor that he was engaged. Might he be lying to her?

The turtle was silent. It didn't say a word to Yasmeena but just stared at her with its vacuous, indifferent eyes. Still, she talked to the turtle, since it had witnessed her "wedding" celebration with Nimr and the blossoming of her body in the light of the tropical sun.

Yasmeena walked around among the pieces of furniture in Nimr's apartment, running her hands over the velvet-upholstered armchairs, the colored telephone, the beautifully papered walls, the gold-plated doorknobs, the bottles of perfume on the dressing table, her new clothes, and the huge, expensive fur that she loved to spread out on the floor and roll around on naked. When she did so, she felt as though she were running through a vast forest full of golden trees and muscular, ebony-skinned men. They would carry her over their heads and throw her back and forth. Then at last she would end up in Nimr's arms, next to his marvelous, beautifully formed body.

She thought, what an amazing, wonderful thing a man's body is! Why don't women notice that? Why do they believe the myth that women are more beautiful? Why don't they look, if only just once, at the beauty of the man's body and the wondrous way it's been put together? He's the most beautiful and magnificent of all the animals in the jungle!

Nimr. Nimr's body. She was growing more and more hungry for him. She would prey on him every night and swallow him up like a female insect that devours the male as they mate. She loved him and didn't feel that he was truly hers anywhere but in bed. She felt secure, and that he was truly united with her, only when he would step inside her body and she, like a fortress, would close her doors around him and hope that he would never leave her. He once confessed to her that he had never found so much pleasure with any other woman and that he was confident of her love for him. If so, then why wouldn't he marry her and allow her to continue floating happily about in the kingdom of his body with its riches and sweet fragrances? She picked up a bottle of cologne to make herself ready to receive him, but it was empty.

She was about to throw it in the wastebasket, but at the last minute, she decided against it. This empty bottle had once been full, containing the days she had spent with him. Fearful that it might bring bad luck to throw it out, she decided to keep it. But then she said to herself, how silly I've become! I collect souvenirs, pictures, empty perfume bottles, and all the idolatrous images of love that I possibly can! How perverted I've gotten to be!

Nimr was late. Men don't know what torment a woman goes through when she's waiting for a man she loves and isn't sure where he's been! Every moment becomes an agonizing march through a field strewn with the mines of her fantasies, for there is nothing more active than the imagination of a jealous woman. She turned to her turtle and said, "When he gets here, I won't ask him where he was. I won't scold him or say anything at all. I'll continue with my plan of waiting and keeping quiet—waiting for the blade of the guillotine to fall on my neck. I know it's there and that it's going to fall, but I can't talk to him about it as long as he keeps on denying it. All I can do is wait to be executed so that I can ask him later, 'Why?'"

The turtle remained silent. Completely silent. It possessed no answers and had no voice. It was one of those rare creatures of nature that is armed with silence. If Yasmeena had bought a cat to keep her company, its meow might have given her a feeling of familiarity or companionship, and if the neighbors were friendlier, she might have had someone whose shoulder she could cry on. But Nimr's apartment was in a fancy, high-class building whose tenants were hostile and predatory. If she'd gotten a dog, it would have talked to her with its whining and yelping. But all Fate had meted out to her was a turtle that evaded her questions by retreating into its shell and that had no answers to give her.

There were no answers. None. Besides, all the answers she might have been given, she already knew. All she had to do was to flee immediately. Run away to Damascus and to her work. Or stay in Beirut and join other working-class folk like herself. Nimr had lapped her up and soon would spit her out. She knew it deep down, and she knew it well. So, let her run away now—now, without wasting another minute.

At the very moment when she realized where she stood, the door opened and in walked Nimr. The thunder rolled again, and she felt small and alone in the face of oppressive forces over which she had no control. She ran to him weeping and threw herself in his arms.

"What's wrong?" he asked. But she didn't reply. "Every night you greet me with tears and silence. You aren't happy anymore. You aren't the Yasmeena I used to know."

She decided not to let him know about her suspicions.

"Nothing's wrong," she said. "Beirut has ruined me, that's all!"

"That's not true," he replied. "You women all accuse Beirut of ruining you when the truth of the matter is that the seeds of corruption were already there deep inside you. All Beirut did was to give them a place to thrive and become visible. It's given them a climate where they can grow."

"But I'm not a whore. I love you. And when our relationship first began you used to allude to marriage."

"What! You're crazy if you think I'd marry a woman who gave herself to me out of wedlock."

"But why not? Didn't you tell me proudly that you'd advised your father to include the issues of equal rights for women in his election platform when he ran for parliament?"

He didn't reply. Instead, he began repeating over and over in a sort of daze, "Me, marry a woman I'd slept with? Who'd already given herself to me?"

"But why not?" Yasmeena insisted. "Or is it that you prefer to be like your friend Nishan—the one you make jokes about all the time because the frigidity of his estimable wife, daughter of the globe-trotting millionaire, led him to announce his preference for men?"

"You think you're smart, don't you? Just shut up!"

He looked furious and agitated. He picked up the empty perfume bottle and fiddled with it for a while without saying anything. Then he threw it in the wastebasket and left the room angrily.

Once he was gone, she leaned down over the wastebasket and took out the empty bottle, then pressed it to her chest, weeping. There was another wild, menacing clap of thunder, and the rain beat on the windows as if it had been sent to carry her away to a land where she'd been doomed to suffer cold, alienation, and homelessness. She had a long cry, then took off her clothes and slipped into bed beside a sleeping Nimr.

She thought, how can he sleep so peacefully? How can a man thrust his spear into the heart of the woman who loves him, then fall fast asleep without feeling scattered and broken in pieces or without getting a splitting headache the way we women do?

When he felt her beside him, he put his arms around her,

and she could feel her body rebelling against her mind. Her body had become an independent republic, destined to be united in an alliance with him. Her body loved him; it loved him, it loved him. The rain was beating threateningly on the windows, and she clung to Nimr's chest. She was drowning, being swept far away by the rain. Meanwhile, Nimr had begun to snore.

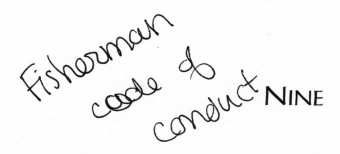
The thunder rolled like a cry of terror whose source was unknown, concealed.

The wind blew fiercely around the unprotected Nighttime Cafe, rocking its proprietor to and fro as he lay on his tattered cot.

Men hovered around the lamp in the center of the room, and the cafe's lone table was lost beneath their large hands, which bore the marks of wounds, fish bites, sea salt, and the night. There was a clap of thunder, and with his disfigured hand, Abu Mustafa pointed to the sea, that black cauldron boiling on the horizon, and said, "It's going to be impossible to fish tonight, lads. So let's go home, and trust God to provide."

Then a voice shouted, "Let's at least make a list of our demands! Somebody bring a pen and paper. Mustafa will write them down for us."

They managed to find a pen, but not a piece of paper. Finally, one of them reached into his chest pocket and took out some food wrapped in a yellow sack. The sack was then opened out to serve as a piece of paper for recording their demands. Along one edge of it there was a large oil stain and the remains of a tomato.

Despite the wind that threatened to blow the paper away, Mustafa managed to write with a trembling hand, "Everything is against us. The sea is polluted, and our fishing methods and equipment are out of date. Consequently, we have to work by night, and most nights of the year we aren't able to fish or go out on the high seas. Besides this, the fish are becoming unhealthy because of the sewage which is poured into the sea. Waste products and garbage, including tin siding, get caught in our nets and cut them with their raw edges, which are as sharp as knives. And these nets are our only source of sustenance."

Coming down in torrents, the rain began to drench both the piece of paper and the men. None of them seemed to care, however, and Mustafa kept on writing: "We're waging a war on all fronts: against nature, against the negligence of the authorities, against poverty. The fisherman is without any sort of security. He is the property of the monopoly-holders, like everything else in this country. They are the ones who buy what we catch, then impose on us whatever prices suit them. There are neither cooperatives for us to join, nor refrigerators in which we can store our catch . . ."

The ill-tempered rain was soaking the piece of paper and obliterating the words that Mustafa had written. Nevertheless, the men persevered, and Mustafa continued to write.

". . . and because we have no cooperatives or refrigerators for storing the fish, we're obliged to sell them at the price imposed on us by Fadhil Salmouni, Faris Sakeeni, and their gang. There are no safeguards or guarantees for the fisherman. He is in constant danger of being maimed or dying on the job, while his wife and children are in danger of finding themselves without a roof over their heads. The fisherman is given no protection nor even the possibility of retirement. He has nothing. . . ."

TEN

The thunder rolled like a cry of terror coming from some hidden, unidentified source.

However, the bey was indifferent to it and simply continued with his telephone conversation, saying, "They've passed the 'Retirement Law' for us as well as for the ministers and ministry heads. . . . Hello? . . . Can you hear me? Hello?"

Fadhil Salmouni hung up the receiver angrily as he muttered and cursed, "We were cut off. Whenever it rains and thunders, the damned phone stops working."

But the abrupt end to the conversation with his friend Abu Nimr didn't bother him. He was quite pleased about the passing of this law, which would ensure the futures of members of parliament, government ministers, and other "protectors of the people" against the vicissitudes of time.

The bey thought about Faiza, who had foretold the passing of the law. This woman knew everything, and he depended on her more than anything. Even during the time when he'd held a ministerial post in the government, he went to her secretly for counsel and advice. Then one day as he was on his way into her house, he ran into the head of the ministry on his way out! They greeted each other with chagrin, like two judges who happen to see each other after hours in the red-light district. They both avoided any mention of the incident. However, it caused a sort of bond to develop between them, the result of which was a political alliance that had positive effects on Fadhil Bey's fortunes thereafter.

He thought to himself that Faiza is nothing but goodness, light, and knowledge! And on this note of good will and folk wisdom, Fadhil Bey got up to get dressed for an evening out. The thunder was still strafing the city, but he didn't appear to notice.

ELEVEN

The ink ran, the paper tore, and the men's throats got dry down at the Nighttime Cafe. They were now soaked to the bone, and when the thunder rolled again, Abu Mustafa was the first to speak, saying, "Let's all go home."

Someone asked, "Who has a lira that I could borrow?"

With a cough, Abu Mustafa replied, "I wish I did!"

Then they all left and were swallowed up by the night.

When Abu Mustafa and his son reached the shack that was their home, the lights were out and everyone was asleep. They went in without any attempt to be quiet, since everyone in their household had gotten used to sleeping through any kind of racket. Such is life for those who live all together in a single room. They don't enjoy the luxury of being disturbed by noise. Twelve people in one room—would it be possible for every one of them to be perfectly quiet even if they were all fast asleep? Mustafa slipped into his accustomed corner, while Abu Mustafa lay down beside his wife, who, as usual, was snoring loudly.

It was nearly pitch black, but Mustafa didn't go straight to sleep. When his mother stopped snoring, his nerves were set on edge, and he knew that they were going to do "that" again. When her breathing grew louder and faster, then blended with his father's moans and gasps, he could feel himself breaking into a sweat. The small room became like a womb of living flesh, and he felt its walls contracting and expanding like the movement of a beating heart. The walls exuded perspiration, and the atmosphere in the room grew hot and feverish. As his hands played the solitary game of madness, his entire body was enveloped by the frenzied heat. Guided by his parents' rhythm, he felt as though he were crawling naked over a bed of hot coals that caused a delicious sting. At last the rain descended, and he felt his body falling limply into a puddle of soft, comforting warmth.

After this, everything grew quiet. The walls returned to their usual place, while the room ceased its throbbing and was drained of its electrically charged fever.

Thought Mustafa, whenever my father is unable to fish and comes home feeling defeated, he goes stalking the golden bird in my mother's gardens. And the result is always a new mouth to feed and the body of a new little child sprawled out in this cramped room of ours. He vents his feelings of rage and despair in bed while I lie here eating my heart out, unable even to talk to the girl I love. There's repression everywhere I go. All I can do in this suffocating atmosphere is to write her love letters and throw them at the entrance to her house where she'll find them when she comes home from school. We exchange letters secretly as if we were spies, and I dream of her on my solitary trips to gardens where the forbidden apple grows. I dream about her with a sense of futility, and in vain I try to caress her with my fingers. Meanwhile, my father returns from his trip without any fish, but with a new baby over his shoulder.

Mustafa couldn't sleep, feeling that everything existed for the express purpose of defeating him and of sabotaging any attempt he might make to escape from the straits of poverty, repression, and subjugation in which he was caught. He felt also that his lone journeys to the valleys of momentary pleasure were going to drive him insane.

He slipped out of bed and left the house. The thunder was beating wickedly in his chest, but he didn't care. He had made a decision, and he was going to carry it out. What he now planned to do seemed to be the only possible solution. He wasn't going to fall into the pit of despair. No, indeed. He wasn't going to fall, nor was he going to die in vain.

He knocked on the door of his friend Nadeem. He knocked for a long time. Then, finally, a sleepy voice answered, "Who is it?"

"Open up, Nadeem. It's Mustafa."

The door creaked as it opened, and a dim light shone out onto the street. Seeing young Mustafa awash in rain, tears, and thunder, Nadeem asked, "What's happened?"

"I'm going to join you. I haven't found any other solution."

"You won't regret it, friend. Welcome."

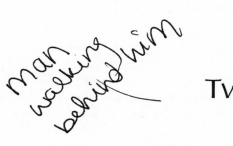

man walking behind him

TWELVE

The thunder rolled like a cry of terror whose origin was shrouded in mystery.

When the lightning had flashed for the second time, Ta'aan turned to look behind him. In the twinkling of an eye, he glimpsed the face of the man who had been walking behind him for hours.

It was then that he concluded: I'm not imagining things. There really is someone following me.

The thunder reverberated again, and his heart nearly burst with fright. As long as this man was following him, he didn't dare go to his brother Nawwaf's house, which had become his hideout. So he kept roaming the streets, avoiding dark or out-of-the-way areas, and he dragged his body from one coffee shop to another, trying all the while to keep from being found alone. Like water running down into a sewer, he felt that he had been poured out onto the city sidewalks and streets. He was incoherent, lost, and terrified.

He thought, there is someone who's going to kill me. When they made the decision in Jaroud to kill me to settle their blood feud, a shot was fired, and all that remains now is for the bullet to land in my body. So one of these nights, I'm destined to get a bullet in me. I wonder exactly where it will lodge itself? In my brain? In my chest? Right in my heart? Or in my gut? Will I bleed to death slowly and painfully? But why should I suffer? Why should I have to die the death of a mangy dog when I haven't committed any crime other than having been able to continue my studies and become a pharmacist? On the day I graduated and took my diploma in hand, little did I know that I was condemning myself to death by execution! What kind of logic is this that guides the clan I was born into? What madness, what insanity is it that rules this world?

On the day Ta'aan had graduated as a pharmacist a few months earlier, he had been eager to get back to Lebanon and begin practicing his profession there. He decided to open a business in Ba'albek called Hanan Pharmacy.

He sent a telegram to his family informing them of his plans and letting them know what day he would be arriving home. However, to his surprise he received a reply from them asking him not to come! They even neglected to congratulate him on getting his degree. Nonplussed by their behavior, he telegrammed them again with his date of return, then got on the next plane to Beirut. When he arrived at the airport, he was taken aback to find that the only people there to meet him were his clan's strongmen, one of whom was an outlaw and fugitive who only appeared in public places in cases of emergency. Each of them held onto him with one hand while keeping the other hand clenched inside his pocket.

Thought Ta'aan, I know—they're holding onto their revolvers. So, is this the kind of reception I get, even though I'm a peaceable person who's never so much as killed an ant?

In fact, he had chosen to become a pharmacist because of his tenderheartedness and sensitivity, which were so extreme that they had prevented him from becoming a surgeon or even a general practitioner. He had hated the sight of blood ever since he was a child. After all, the first thing he had ever laid eyes on was a pool of blood, the blood of his slain paternal uncle. What had happened to make these men come to meet him at the airport bearing the scent of blood and destruction?

Once they were in the car, he asked his father about it, and he listened dumbfounded as his father explained to him how he had been sentenced to death for the crime of obtaining a university degree!

"Your cousin Mur'ib killed a member of the Khardaliyya clan to avenge the death of your uncle. It so happened that the slain member of the other clan held a university degree, so when they decided to take vengeance, they stipulated that the victim be the first young man of our clan to graduate from the

64

university. And that happened to be you. This is the new clan tradition with regard to taking blood vengeance. If my mother were to kill someone of another clan, vengeance would have to be taken by killing my mother, and the death of an educated person can only be avenged by killing an educated person from the other tribe."

Ta'aan thought gloomily, so the clan's thinking has been influenced by technology, and now they appreciate the value of getting an education!

Pausing briefly in front of the pillars of the Hamra Cinema on Hamra Street, he pretended to light a cigarette while he tried to ascertain whether the man was still following him. It was still pouring down rain, and the last remains of the summer heat were coming to an end. He felt a sort of ill-defined distress inside. He longed for a woman, for love. He missed swimming, hanging around without anything in particular to do, sitting in cafes, and listening to the laughter of pretty young women whose whole demeanor was an invitation to love and madness. He was tired of having to walk down the streets fearfully, looking over his shoulder every two seconds like a mafia movie hero. He was tiring of carrying around a revolver that he didn't even know how to use, of hiding in his brother Nawwaf's house and bolting the doors shut. He was tired of keeping the curtains drawn and having to avoid standing in front of windows.

He was tired of being unemployed and of waiting for the death that was coming but didn't come. He was tired, weary, spent. He began to tremble, and he didn't feel strong enough to remain standing up. The cigarette fell out of his hand. The man wasn't pursuing him.

Or, he wondered, might I be imagining things? I think that every man I see in the street is after me! My nerves are shot. I've got to get back to my hideout. I've got to . . .

He flagged down the first taxi he saw. He got in and gave the driver his address like someone who is revealing some weighty secret. Actually, he didn't give him his address, but only the name of the street. He would walk the rest of the way to his brother's house and make sure that no one followed him from the taxi. He turned to look behind him and saw a river of car headlights flashing on and off. He stared at them in horror. He imagined that every one of those cars was full of men sitting with their fingers on the triggers of their machine guns, and that the moment he got out of the taxi, his body would be riddled with bullets. He would quiver as he fell, as though he were dancing, and if he escaped death in the street and managed to get into bed alive that night, he would be besieged by nightmares. Then he'd wake up to the sound of bullets mowing him down along with his brother and his brother's children. The men would kill everyone in the house, and his brother Nawwaf would fall down dead before he'd had time to fire a single shot.

The taxi came to a stop. Ta'aan got out and noticed that there was more than one car parked in the street. So, was more than one person following him? But, he reasoned, the streets are for everyone! The fact that a car is parked on the street where I'm hiding doesn't necessarily mean that the person driving it wants to kill me! No. But "they" do want to kill me! That I know. I died on the day they sentenced me to death to avenge a man that I didn't kill, that I had no part in killing, and whose face I've never even seen before. Yet here I am, dragging my body around for the duration of the futile days remaining to me.

He began walking, trying his utmost to make his steps calm and steady. However, it was no use, and his trembling legs took off with rapid strides. Then he heard the sound of footsteps behind him. He sped up, and so did the footsteps. He tightened his grip on the revolver in his pocket. He was certain that someone was pursuing him and that his pursuer was gaining on him. Whoever it was came closer and put his hand on Ta'aan's shoulder. There was no more room for doubt now. Without knowing what he was doing, Ta'aan drew his gun, turned, and shot the man. Just like that, without a word.

The man fell to the ground. For the first time, Ta'aan glimpsed his face and saw a look full of bewilderment and alarm in his eyes. He had just murdered someone. He'd killed a man whom he'd never laid eyes on before, and the victim seemed utterly taken by surprise.

THIRTEEN

The thunder rolled like a cry of terror whose source was shrouded in mystery.

Farah extricated himself from the girl's body. Despite the cold and the rain that pounded on the windows, his entire body was dripping with perspiration. There was another clap of thunder, and she said, "Try again!"

He lit a cigarette and didn't say anything. He couldn't tell her that there was no use in trying. After all, before her there had been another woman in the same bed, and before her another, and he'd failed with every one of them. Seven women in one week, a different one every day, and he hadn't been able to "come" with a single one of them.

He thought ruefully, even my own body and soul don't belong to me anymore, so how could I possibly hold sway over anyone else's?

He, the one that even a cow or a sheep would have been unsafe around in his village, could no longer perform even with the most beautiful woman. With the kind of phony sensitivity and tenderness that women put on in such situations, she said, "I love you! Please try again. I've waited so long for this moment. I used to think about it whenever I saw you on television or clipped pictures of you out of magazines and newspapers and used them to decorate my bedroom walls. Come, my love, you 'singer of manliness'!"

When Farah heard her address him by his title, "singer of manliness," he nearly burst out laughing and crying at the same time. It was with this image that Nishan had launched him to stardom: the "singer of manliness" with the perfect male physique, thick chest hair that peeked out through the neck opening of his shirt, and a husky, rustic voice that was the furthest thing from affectation or effeminacy. And the young women of Beirut fell for him hook, line, and sinker. He aroused in them a longing for the age of strong men, men who were too virile to be affected or unnatural or to bow to the demands of social protocol, but who were close to the common people, to the wildflowers, and to the ears of grain in the field—men who would slap their women with one hand and embrace them tenderly with the other.

Nishan had said that there was a hunger in Beirut for "the man's man" and that he would employ Farah to serve his own interests. Thus it was that he forced Farah to play the role of the "tough, irascible man," while inside he was haunted by feelings of delicacy, fragility, and fear. The "singer of manliness" indeed! Whenever he opened to the first page of some magazine and saw a picture of himself with this title as a caption beneath it, he wanted to both laugh and cry. He thought back to the first time Nishan had called him by this name.

We were together in his private chalet, and on that serene, cloudless day, the autumn sea stretched out before me in a bewitching, delightful way. Like everyone from Damascus and its environs, I'm in love with the sea, and in my mind's eye I pictured young women's naked bodies covering the sand all summer long. Like all the men in the world, I love women with a passion.

The dining-room table in the chalet was piled high with delicious food and drink, and the wine had gone to my head along with the autumn sun, which was still hot despite the cool breeze. The effects of wine are multiplied several times over when one is sitting in the sunshine, and I didn't know for certain whether I was intoxicated with alcohol or with life. Nishan was studying me with a stern look on his face. I remembered what he had said about "obedience," and I made up my mind to do everything he said to merit this sunny day on the beach with all its pleasures and delights. So under "orders" from Nishan, I lay down for a while on the balcony of the chalet, since he'd said that a bronze-like tan was a "must" for being attractive and that, consequently, sunbathing was part of my job. Actually, I'd been hoping to go running along the beach, free and unhindered like a happy stallion, but he insisted that the required tan had to be gotten according to a strict schedule. So for fifteen minutes I'd be stretched out on my stomach, then fifteen minutes on my back, and so on. I was forbidden to bend my body so that there wouldn't remain white patches of skin anywhere. And every once in a while he would come along and rub me with suntan oil.

I was lying on my stomach when he began to massage my back for me, causing the aroma of the costly suntan oil to diffuse through the air. At first his fingers moved gently and delicately back and forth over my skin, like the fingers of a blind man running his hands over the body of the woman he loves. But then his touch became rough and violent, like a plow going down into the soil. And then I understood.

In bed I was both inebriated and confused. It wasn't enjoyable. However, it also wasn't as unpleasant as I'd imagined it would be. For the sake of wealth, fame, glory, and a life of freedom and ease, anything goes. Nishan's thick, flabby flesh quivered with amorous passion as he said, "Women aren't able to give me this kind of pleasure, you magnificent man! I'm going to call you 'the singer of manliness.' With a man I feel intimate and familiar, whereas with 'them' I feel alienated and estranged. It gives me pleasure to be united with a person whom I know and can talk to, someone I feel can understand me. I don't understand women, and they don't understand me, so as far as I'm concerned, it makes no difference whether I screw a woman or a goat—it's all the same. But men are something else."

It seemed to me that he was trying to justify himself, and I felt pity for him. But something inside me was breaking, shattering, and I was no longer the master of my own soul. I had sold it once and for all—to the devil!

The thunder rumbled again.

Farah's cigarette had burned all the way down. He reached out to get another one, then remembered that Nishan had forbidden him to smoke.

The young woman had finished getting dressed. As she headed for the door there was a look of invitation in her eyes, a look that said that if he called her back, she would be willing to take her clothes off all over again and give it another try. But he didn't.

He let her go. And when she had closed the door behind her, he felt as though the door between him and the world of women had been shut forever.

FOURTEEN

"I'm going to steal the statue." That was the decision Abu'l-Malla had come to after long agonizing.

The fact of the matter was that stealing the statue wasn't going to be difficult, since the site where the archaeological excavations were being done was full of gold and silver treasures that were being moved elsewhere one by one, whereas the clay and marble pieces that remained had been left in the small hut which was being guarded by Abu'l-Malla. So practically speaking, it wouldn't be hard to steal the statue. The hard part was convincing himself to do such a thing. He had lived his entire life content with his lot, performing the ritual prayers and striving, above all, to lead a life of piety and to maintain a clear conscience. Even poverty wasn't a cause of great suffering for him, since he believed that one of the unquestionable facts of existence was that, as told in the Muslim holy book, some people will be elevated by degrees above others.

But now he had changed. The change had begun when life's overwhelming demands had obliged him to send his third daughter to work as a live-in domestic servant. Ever since he'd set foot in that mansion in Beirut's Hazmiyyeh district where he had left her, a thorn had grown up in his heart and had begun to relentlessly tear him to pieces. When he came away from the Hazmiyyeh neighborhood with its luxurious mansions and returned to his own neighborhood of tinplate shacks, it seemed as though he were seeing the place for the first time. The walls and roofs of the houses were made of tinplate, and in the winter, the rain dripped down from the roof of his one-roomed house onto his few shabby possessions. No running water. No windows. Just flies, poverty, children's screams and shouts, and women's reprimands, curses, and insults.

The thunder rolled. He said to himself, I'm going to steal that statue.

He would steal the statue and get his daughters back. Why should he hand it over to the museum if he could sell it himself and use the money to redeem his daughters out of their misery? He remembered the lectures that had been given by an engineer during the days when he still worked on the excavation site. At that time he'd been as strong as a horse. He hadn't yet been afflicted with the heart ailment that he suffered from now.

The engineer had said, "These are the ancient monuments of your great homeland, Lebanon. Uncover them carefully and protect them from being stolen or damaged during the dig. They're your history."

His homeland? Even though he'd been born in Lebanon and would die there, his nationality was still listed on his personal identification card as "under investigation." His history? All he knew was his miserable present. Three of his daughters had gone to work in the mansions of the wealthy, and even with the wages earned by his working sons, he wasn't able to make ends meet.

"I'm going to steal the statue."

The statue had wide-set eyes that peered at him with a malevolent, frightening look of derision.

When Nadeem Effendi, the assistant to the site director, saw the statue, he said to Abu'l-Malla, "This is a rare work of art, more valuable than all the gold statues that we've found along the shore."

After this, he expected them to waste no time moving it elsewhere as they'd done with the other valuable pieces. But then Nadeem Effendi seemed suddenly to forget about the statue. It was left sitting across from Abu'l-Malla all day long, staring at him with that sinister, contemptuous look. He even began carrying on conversations with it. He told it about how he'd taken his daughter to the mansion in Hazmiyyeh and how he'd suddenly been afflicted with his heart disease. Then he started relating to it everything that happened to him and everything that was on his mind. As for the statue, it would listen to him attentively without interrupting. Then it would answer him, yet without offering him any solace or comfort. It seemed angry somehow, and there was something in its tone of voice that goaded Abu'l-Malla to take some action.

Once he asked it straight out, "What do you want me to do?"

The statue answered, "I want you to do whatever you're told by the true voices inside you. Search for them. Listen to them. Welcome them and be willing to die on their behalf. Do you call 'life' what you and your children are living now?"

Thus it was that a peculiar relationship developed between Abu'l-Malla and the statue. He began to greet it every morning when he came into the hut, and they even talked about the weather. Once Abu'l-Malla asked the statue about its life story, but no sooner had it begun recounting it to him than some workers came and it fell silent. A rumor began circulating at the dig site that Abu'l-Malla talked to himself and that more than one person had heard him.

Someone approached Abu'l-Malla one day with a tempting offer which he immediately rejected. He asked Abu'l-Malla to steal the statue in return for a fantastic sum—ten thousand Lebanese pounds. Ten thousand pounds! Nevertheless, he refused to sell his statue friend, in spite of the quarreling and bickering that sometimes arose between them. After all, the statue was the only one who listened to him or showed any interest in conversing with him. Ignoring Abu'l-Malla's initial refusal, the man said to him, "I'll be back the day after tomorrow. All you have to do is carry it home in your coat pocket. It won't cost you a thing—in fact, you'll get ten thousand pounds out of the deal. But don't say a word about this to anyone, or else!"

As the man finished his statement, he ran his finger across his neck, making sounds with his mouth like that of someone's throat being slit. Abu'l-Malla got the point.

When Nadeem Effendi came back the next time, Abu'l-Malla asked him anxiously, "When are you planning to move this statue to the museum? I'm afraid to be responsible for it."

Nadeem Effendi replied nonchalantly, "Oh, the statue? I'd forgotten about it. Right, we'll move it soon. It just requires some planning and organization."

So, he would steal the statue.

He would carry it home with him that very night, and later the man would come to get it.

He was going to steal the statue.

And the thunder rolled.

He reached out toward the statue, his hand trembling, and felt afraid. Suddenly, the statue seemed like a giant to him, while he himself seemed tiny and frail. But no sooner had he grasped it and begun to pick it up than his heart began to race, and he was possessed by a sense of superhuman strength. This was the first time in his life that he had broken a law, defied a system, or committed any forbidden act. He felt a tremendous rush of pleasure all over his body and the delirious ecstasy born of possessing infinite strength. The statue remained silent. However, frightening beams of light emanated from its eyes. Or was it just the reflection of the lightning?

He put the statue in his pocket and began pressing it rapturously against his body. All the other statues in the hut began swaying back and forth, quivering, moaning, and throbbing. Oh!

A few minutes later Abu'l-Malla collapsed on a nearby seat with a sort of warm, sticky feeling all over. He felt his heart beating more rapidly, and he was filled with an amazing vitality and energy. He hadn't felt so lively since his heart attack. His heart still pounding wildly, he continued in this state of tension all the way back to his neighborhood of tinplate shacks. From now on he was going to acquaint himself with the path of pleasure and enjoyment—he was going to live. He would steal again. He would try everything before it was too late. He would try his hand at murder as well. He'd never killed anyone before, but he'd give it a try. He would have given anything, even his life, to be able to relive the amazing sensation that he'd experienced at the moment he took hold of the statue. It was as if he had made love to Bilqees, Queen of Sheba, whose tales are recounted by storytellers.

In his tinplate hovel he lay down with the statue beside him. His wife and children were at the house of some neighbors who had bought a television a few days earlier. He thought to himself, what peculiar folks we are here in this neighborhood! We buy a television when we don't even have an inside toilet!

In any case, it was better for his family to be out of the house. He needed to be alone until the man came to get the statue and pay him his ten thousand pounds. However, the statue still stared with disdainful malice at Abu'l-Malla, whose heart continued to beat like a wild drum. He was frightened somewhat by the way the statue looked at him. If only that man would come quickly and get it over with! He decided to get up and cover the statue so that he wouldn't be able to see it. However, he was unable to rise, frozen in place, paralyzed by the rays being emitted by the statue's eyes.

"Forgive me," he said to it apologetically, "but you're the one who urged me to do something—to rise up and rebel. It was the only thing I could do!"

He saw the statue grow larger and larger, then get down onto the floor. With its now gigantic body, it approached him in a rage. Abu'l-Malla tried to scream but couldn't find his voice. His breathing quickened and his heart was about to burst. The statue then reached out and began to place its fingers around his neck.

My God! It's trying to strangle me! It wants to kill me!

Still, however, he couldn't get a single cry for help to come out of his mouth. He saw the statue's stony fingers encircle his neck. Then he felt it press harder and harder and harder. He gasped and gasped, then . . . he gasped no more.

Later, Umm al-Malla came back to their hut to find that her husband had breathed his last. She began to scream and wail, and the neighbors came running. As for his young children, they found on the floor beside their dead father a strange-looking stone doll. It smiled at them, so they picked it up, took it outside, and played with it until they got tired of it, after which it ended up in a mud puddle among the tinplate huts.

When his son al-Malla, who worked as a welder, came

home that night and found that his father had died of a blood clot—or so everyone thought—he noticed what looked like fingerprints on his neck. However, he attributed them to his father's attempt to unbutton his shirt collar when the heart attack came over him. Weeping in sorrow, he said, "It was his patient endurance of poverty that killed him!"

He then aimed the flame of his welding iron at the roof. The oxygen ignited, producing a brilliant tongue of fire which caused the tinplate roof to melt. But the wind blew in through the hole, so he turned off the welding iron and collapsed into a sitting position, with his hands hanging limply at his sides, as if he didn't know what to do with them. His gaze was fixed on the hole that opened onto the sky, which was a solid roof of gloomy blackness. Not a single star could be seen twinkling through the opening. The rain then began to leak through, its drops falling onto Abu'l-Malla's corpse right over the heart, drop by drop, as if the night were bleeding.

death by statue

FIFTEEN

It continued to rain and rain.

Yasmeena wondered to herself, how long can my heart endure this torment before it explodes?

Meanwhile, it poured and poured.

She was stretched out on a soft, white rabbit-fur rug, and her turtle was sitting nearby with its head inside its shell.

Yasmeena thought, the turtle escapes being skinned, then sits here on top of the hide of a skinned rabbit! The rabbit can run faster than the turtle, but what's the use of running when every step leads to harm of some sort?

Perhaps that was why she had decided to "play turtle" with Nimr. No longer was she the jasmine flower of Damascus who spread her sweet aroma, gaiety, and songs everywhere she went, confident that the world would embrace her love and love her in return. There were other "equations" in control of this city which would lead to destruction for anyone who dared to give spontaneously. Whoever ran like the rabbit toward his goal would be hunted down and flayed. Everything in this city was teaching her to be a turtle. The turtle is silent and knows when to conceal its head and its thoughts, and this was how she, too, had become. But unlike the turtle's, her shell was stuffed with torment, agony, and suffering.

It kept on raining and raining.

She felt as though she were naked beneath skewers of piercing rain, stripped of everything but her love and her weakness, resigned to her fate like a genie escorting itself to its own annihilation. Nimr's wedding date was now set. He hadn't told her so directly, but she'd read the notice in the newspaper, and that night she'd read in his eyes an anticipation of her questions or at least her tears. Nevertheless, she had made up her mind to remain the turtle because of her love for him.

She thought to herself, people of his social class seem to hate candor! Everything in their velvet-smooth surroundings is a kind of poker game. Whoever shows his cards first, loses. Emotions here aren't emotions. They're a game of tug-of-war. And a love relationship is between two people in which each one bites the other, and whoever screams first, loses.

But she wasn't going to scream first. She wasn't going to lose. She couldn't bear to lose him, but instead would fight as silently as possible to keep him for as long as possible.

And it rained and rained.

The Carl Orff music she had put on tore her to pieces as a predator tears its prey. The turtle's game didn't suit her; she'd been made simply to love and give, not to "play" love as if it were a game of chess.

Meanwhile, it rained and rained.

The music was a river of madness, and the room was drowning in a sea of colors and frenzied, invisible breaths. Then suddenly, the turtle got up off the rabbit-skin rug, took off her shell, and stood up naked, stretching in blissful enjoyment of her body. And as she did so, she became transparent and began to dance and dance. Then she began to fly through the room, singing and bumping up against the windows as she searched for a way out.

she's a bird/butterfly again

the only positive non-human character

Sixteen

As Nimr drove his car to where she was, it rained and rained.

Might I actually love her? he wondered.

Is it possible for me, Nimr Faris Sakeeni, to love? Me, love a poor girl who's ignorant of social etiquette, has bad taste in clothes, and gave herself to me physically without our being married? Love, love, love—that's all she understands or talks about. For me, there are sexual relations, in which there's nothing wrong with leading a woman on with the word "love," and then there is a marital relation, in which the most important thing is that the marriage be politically and financially expedient for my father and me. All the whores I've ever slept with have talked about love, but this one is the most persistent about it. Might she have believed her own lie? Does she imagine that she really does love me and that love actually exists?

But if I've rejected her completely, if she doesn't strike any forgotten chord inside me, then why should I care what happens to her? Why don't I just throw her out of the house and be rid of her?

Love her? In the way she gives to me, I smell a fragrance that I've never known before. Or am I just afraid that she's sincere in her love, so sincere that she might commit suicide and cause me a scandal?

But why all this meaningless talk anyway? Never before have I wasted my time thinking about women or their affairs! I think about them when I'm with them, but their physical presence is the only thing that draws me to them. When I'm away from them, they have no existence for me. Besides, I have other things to worry about. I've got enough problems at work because of that fisherman, Mustafa! Ever since that boy joined the fishermen, I've had one headache after another. Keeping the fishermen in line isn't easy like it used to be. They've started using dangerous words like "dignity," "rights," and "justice." The bastards!

Love?

Even if it were love, I wouldn't have time for such a thing. And if I were to be lenient with Yasmeena and understanding of her feelings, then I might end up being the same way with Mustafa and with everyone else around me. And in that case, I'd lose my reputation, my position, and my fortune. No. The only thing that binds me to her is that she's luscious in bed!

It kept raining and raining.

He stopped at a red light and was approached by a young boy who was out begging in spite of the rain. Irritated, Nimr took off even though the light was still red.

True, she's appetizing in bed—and she's that way because of her own appetite for me. She isn't a graduate of some sex institute in Stockholm, but she has an incredible feel for what a man's body wants, as if she'd been trained in the art for years. She's a master at draining me to the dregs, like some concubine who'd received long training in the palaces of Umayyad sultans. Maybe it's in her blood. Maybe Damascene women, true to their reputation, inherit the knowledge of how to enjoy a man and how to give him enjoyment from their mothers, passing it down from one generation to the next. I don't think I'll give her up permanently. Instead, I'll turn her over to Nishan for a while and stay away from her after I'm first married to avoid a scandal. Then I'll come back to her. That damned Nishan; I wish he'd wrap up the agreement—she's in utter despair. I hope he'll dazzle her with his wealth. After all, despite all her claims about how important love is, I know she loves money, too, and would submit to anything under threat of poverty. But can I blame her? I love money, too; otherwise, I wouldn't have agreed to marry Naila, that imbecilic squirrel!

∾

When Nimr got home he expected to walk into a nice warm apartment. Instead, he found all the windows open, the wind blowing in wildly, and Yasmeena standing in front of one of the windows in her flimsy white gown, like a butterfly getting ready to fly.

"What's the matter with you?" Nimr asked angrily.

In a dreamy voice, Yasmeena said, "The turtle flew away!"

"You crazy woman!" he shouted. "Why did you throw it out the window?"

"I didn't," she replied. "I told you it flew away. It discovered its wings and flew away!"

Angrier now than before, he said, "Get your clothes on. Now. We're going to the big party that Nishan's having at his house tonight. He might make you into a movie star. Who knows?"

Nishan's secret apartment was like a seashell full of madness, wine, music, and wild clamor. Everything in it was quaking and dancing, even the lights.

Someone was doing finger paintings on the body of a naked woman, and cries of approval would go up whenever he drew the right shape in the right spot. A second unclad woman was swimming around in a huge marble flowerpot filled with champagne, and in another part of the room, two naked women danced together, one of them black and the other "platinum." Among the guests were men of the type whose pictures one sees in magazines, talking over the din around them, engrossed in their conversation, indifferent to all the naked women who were poured out onto the floor like brackish water in the streets.

Business is business, thought Nimr to himself. Work comes first. In a race of wolves there isn't any place for love or mercy. If any of them allows itself to be weak, the rest of the pack will devour it and continue on its way.

As Nimr introduced Yasmeena to Nishan, he felt stern and resolute despite a barely perceptible feeling of discomfort somewhere deep inside. Thinking it to be indigestion, he decided not to go overboard on drinking that night.

Nishan extended his hand, which was adorned with a large

diamond that confirmed what a very important businessman he was. And when he shook Yasmeena's hand, his bloated, flaccid hand felt to her like a slimy, dead frog.

She started with fright. It was the first time in her life that she had seen such a place. It was also the first time that Nimr had accompanied her to this world of wantonness and dissipation rather than keeping her to himself. So this was the end. She decided to go find a place where she could be alone. So, claiming that she needed to spruce herself up, she excused herself from the two men and ran to the bathroom.

No sooner had she left than the two men burst into collusive laughter. Imitating Nimr's tone of voice, Nishan parroted, "'Thank you for your unexpected invitation!' What a smooth liar you've become! I almost said to you, 'But the whole party was put on just for you to deliver the goods!' Pardon me, I mean, the mademoiselle. Mademoiselle? The one who for three months has been scampering about your bed like a gazelle, without resting for a second! Pleased to meet you, mademoiselle!"

They laughed again. Then, somewhat proudly, Nimr asked, "So, what do you think of her?"

Nishan replied scornfully, "She's a bit fat. She doesn't know how to dress or how to move. She looks like a tenth-rate singer who's inherited a fortune but doesn't know the meaning of elegance. That plunging neckline shows what lousy taste she has."

"But she's got a very exciting bosom!"

"You know I'm not interested in her boobs. Women hold no fascination for me. All she'd be asked to do would be to accompany Farah and me in public places—nothing more. To keep up appearances. The only requirement is that she know how to dress well. But as far as I can see, the only thing she knows how to do well is undress, which is a service I wouldn't be asking of her!"

With the harshness of one accustomed to dealing with fishermen and keeping them in their place, Nimr said, "All right then, are you going to take her, or shall I look for another friend who'll do me this service?"

By this time the two men had shed all pretense of pleasantness. Gone was the smoothness of their silk neckties and expensive cologne, and their eyes gleamed like those of two men fighting inside a mine. So with equal severity Nishan replied, "I'll take her on one condition—that you get your future father-in-law, Fadhil Bey Salmouni, to make the bid fall to me. One good turn deserves another. Your Yasmeena holds no allure for me, but for strictly practical purposes I'm willing to take her on as a mistress for a while."

"Of course. The first thing I'll do after the wedding is to make certain the deal is concluded to your satisfaction, and . . ."

". . . and take her back. You still seem to want her somehow."

Their conversation ended abruptly when Yasmeena returned, her lips painted a garish red.

Nishan felt repulsed as he looked at her. He thought to himself, how disgusting women are! They leave mascara and lipstick stains on the pillow and generally soil the sheets with other things as well. Men, on the other hand, are handsome and clean and don't leave a filthy mess behind them. Man is without a doubt the most beautiful, magnificent animal in all of nature. However, the necessities of work require that I flirt with this cow. So be it, then. Like they say, "Business is business." I'll build my empire by any means necessary.

He was oppressed by the penetrating aroma of the perfume that had been wafting over from Yasmeena since her return, in spite of all the other smells that permeated the place along with the music.

He said to her amiably, "What marvelous perfume you're wearing!"

Without thinking, she responded to his compliment by taking out her perfume bottle and pouring some on his hand. He recoiled like someone who has just been bitten by an adder. This little cow obviously couldn't comprehend how much he loved his body and what tender care he took of it! Knowing that perfume irritates the skin, he used it only in the form of a spray, and even then only on his clothes. She wasn't the least bit perceptive, as if her senses didn't work properly—except in bed, perhaps. But that didn't interest him in the least. Farah dominated all his passions—Farah, with his strong, village-boy's body.

Nimr asked him, "What's the latest news on the star that your public-relations firm launched recently?"

Taken aback somewhat, Nishan replied, "Oh, uh, he's stupendous. His first recording made record sales, and his concert in Aley raked in fantastic profits. He's like putty in my hands. His only shortcoming is that he used to be a philosophy buff. But before long he'll recover from the malady of excessive thinking and sensitivity!"

SEVENTEEN

The spray of the waves washed the men's faces as the Magic Lantern plowed ahead toward the open seas. Mustafa couldn't pinpoint a reason for his vague feeling of distress, but at least he no longer grieved for the fish of the sea. It wasn't that the bond between him and other creatures had been severed. It was simply lying dormant, superseded by another bond which tied him to those who, like him and his father, were suffering members of the species of "terrestrial fish," those lost in the cruel underside of life in Beirut, like fish that had been forced to swim in its sewer lines despite their longing for freedom, sunshine, and clean, fresh water. He was now preoccupied with the war against the Sakeeni and Salmouni families and others of their class, who were stealing what few morsels the poor had to sustain themselves straight out of their mouths. His once-romantic ears were no longer attuned to the moans of the fish caught in the nets. Instead, they pricked up at the sound of the moans of people around him, his own pained groaning, and the plaintive cries of the men who braved the dangers of the sea and the night while Nimr Sakeeni and his lot dozed on their yachts.

His father, for example, the great "fish of fatigue," had been flushed with fever since morning, and the blood that he was coughing up was no longer pink, but bright red. Not only that, but his obsession with the magic lantern had turned into outright madness; he was now convinced that he would meet the genie before he died. Mustafa had tried in vain to convince his father not to come out tonight. However, not only had he insisted on coming out, but he'd also brought with him the forbidden sticks of dynamite. He was dying and out of his mind.

What a night it was! It was the first time his father had fished with dynamite since the accident in which he'd lost his fingers.

Mustafa looked at his father pensively. He could make his face out despite the relative darkness, and he saw sweat pouring off his features, like a gambler who in a single stroke has risked everything he owns. Abu Mustafa was gambling with fate and with the wind, playing roulette with the sea.

Yes, indeed. His father had the face of a gambler, especially tonight. . . . Perhaps it was on account of the fever, or perhaps it was something else!

Abu Mustafa was completely silent. This was to be the night of a lifetime, the night when he made the strike in which he would either lose or win, once and for all. All his life he had been certain that the genie and the magic lamp were close at hand, and that someday he would surely catch them in his net. Then all his wishes would come true, and inner peace and joy would be his. And today, more than ever before, he felt the genie's nearness to him. The more perforated his lungs had become during the past month, the more vividly he had perceived the genie's nearness and essence, as it became somehow inseparable from him.

For thirty years he'd been running over the waves in search of the genie. For thirty years he had been casting his nets, then running his fingers through their contents in hopes of finding the lamp!

He was feverish, so feverish. Yet he sensed that the lamp was near, so near that true knowledge and understanding were about to become his and that their meeting was inevitable, destined to take place. After all, he'd spent a lifetime striving for this very thing.

He cast his nets, then lit the fuse of the dynamite. He lit the entire bundle all at once, and before he could hear the protests of his son and the other men, he had jumped along with it into the water. Now his whole body was a bundle of dynamite whose purpose was to catch the lamp.

The explosion rang out along with Mustafa's scream. The water was thrown into a roiled, raging tumult, then all at once, everything grew calm. The waves were dyed a black hue, and on the surface of the water a mangled corpse could be seen floating among the shredded nets. As the men brought the nets in, Abu Mustafa's body came up with them like a rare fish spattered with blood, mingled with bits and pieces of clothing and other unidentified, broken objects and remains. Among the debris Mustafa thought he saw the fragments of a very, very old lamp. Or might they just have been some of his father's blood-washed bones? He also thought he saw a column of smoke and ashes slowly ascend from his father's remains, then vanish into the cold, dark emptiness, like the smoke of a genie before its final disappearance. In a flash of insight that could hardly be doubted, he cried out mournfully to his father's mangled corpse, "But *you're* the one who never learned how to come out of the bottle! What you were looking for wasn't in the depths of the sea, but deep inside you!"

And he burst into tears.

death by dynamite

EIGHTEEN

The lawyer said to Ta'aan, "Your situation is very bad. You killed a man you didn't know without any justification!"

"I killed him in self-defense."

"But he was unarmed!"

"I killed him because he was one of *them*. He wanted to find out where I was hiding in order to kill me."

"But he was a foreign tourist. Maybe he was lost and was trying to ask you for directions."

"Impossible!"

"While he lay dying in the hospital, he said that he'd asked you for directions and that you had answered him with a bullet!"

"Oh, my God!"

Ta'aan's head fell between his hands. So they had succeeded in killing him after all, in a manner of speaking. They had wanted to kill him to avenge a man whose face he had never seen before, and as a consequence, they had driven him to *kill* a man whose face he had never seen before! And now they were dragging him to the gallows to be killed by a man whose face he would never see!

death by punishment
the stranger is important

NINETEEN

The moment Farah awoke, he heard a voice screaming at him from somewhere deep inside, "Flee . . . run! Leave everything and go back to your village! Run!"

In spite of the sleeping pills he'd taken, he hadn't slept well. In fact, he hadn't been able to sleep since he'd lost his ability to pray or to make love to women. He'd also begun hearing voices that came from somewhere inside him. It was as if they were his own voice, yet not his own voice. He would find himself answering them out loud, and even Nishan had warned him against the habit of talking to himself. He no longer slept, but he no longer woke up, either. He was in a continual nightmare that was neither reality nor illusion nor life. What he was living bore some resemblance to life, yet wasn't life.

He remembered that he had to go to the barber that day to buy a toupee for his new television-show contract, then to the tailor, then to lunch with Nishan at the ritzy Loukoulous Restaurant. After that, he'd take his tranquilizers again in order to sleep so that he'd be ready for the New Year's Eve party later that night. When he became aware of his schedule for the day, he was suddenly gripped with an intense anguish. He thought to himself, I don't want to live through this day.

Instead of drinking the glass of milk that the servant had brought him, he poured himself a glass of whiskey. He gulped it down with a couple of sleeping pills, then went back to bed, having made up his mind to sleep through to the following morning.

TWENTY

Farah sat half-drugged in the luxurious Loukoulous Restaurant. In spite of the cold shower, Nishan's slaps, and the upper that he'd swallowed, he still felt dizzy. Nishan had dragged him out of bed like a puppy, making it clear that he'd bet on him and wasn't going to let him drop out of the race. He slapped him, then kissed him, then slapped him, then kissed him, then ordered him to get dressed and dragged him to the fancy restaurant, where they were scheduled to meet with the producer of Farah's first film.

Here he was, eating the fancy food that for so long he'd seen pictures of in magazines and had dreamed of eating someday, but it had no more taste to him than a handful of straw.

The young woman sitting at the table with them was silent. Nishan introduced her to him as "Mademoiselle Yasmeena." He stared at her bleary-eyed. It seemed to him that he'd see her before. But where . . . where . . . where? He didn't remember anymore.

Meanwhile, she stared back at him, trying to remember where she'd seen him, but her thoughts kept scattering and going back to Nimr. Where might he be now? And with whom? Who was he smiling at and gracing with his fair-skinned radiance? Was everything over between them? Would she have to stay with Nishan until he turned her over to another man, then to another, then another?

Farah said to her, "It seems I've seen you somewhere before, Mademoiselle Yasmeena!"

She replied, "And I also feel as though I've seen you before."

Then, as she gazed out the window at Beirut, she added, "How lovely this city is from a distance!"

To which Farah replied in a whisper, "Exactly! From a distance . . . from a distance!"

After this they exchanged no more conversation, which was left from then on to Nishan and the producer. Instead, they watched what was taking place in silent misery, while from their presence there emanated an aura of bewitched fascination, like that of moths at the moment they are consumed by the heat of a flame around which they've hovered too closely.

They didn't recall that they had been travel companions in the taxi which had brought them to Beirut only a few months earlier.

They had become two very different people.

TWENTY-ONE

Today she would have to decide: either to move in with Nishan or return to a life of poverty. She paced around Nimr's luxurious flat. There was nothing that frightened her as much as poverty. Besides, during the past few months she'd grown accustomed to a life of ease, and now, after having gotten a taste of yachts, chalets, and caviar, she no longer felt able to go back to her former life of toil and drudgery.

It was a beautiful, sunny day, so she went out for a walk in hopes of finding herself. Instead, all she found was terror.

It was disturbing to see the poor crowded into an abandoned lot—abandoned, that is, by everything but refuse— surrounded by the mansions of the White Sands district, especially in view of the fact that they'd come there on a pleasure outing! Terrifying, also, was the sight of the crowds along the coastal road, where people were sprawled out on the ground, eating sunflower seeds and spitting out the shells, listening to transistor radios, and watching their children do somersaults on the filthy pavement.

She saw a pregnant woman chasing her two young children while her potbellied husband sat on a tumble-down chair staring out to sea and smoking his water pipe. This was the best she could expect if she married someone of her own class. She wasn't willing to turn into a woman who subsisted on vexation and discontent, the screaming of children, and the snoring of an exhausted husband. She couldn't live without shudders of delight, a huge, fur-covered bed, furtive kisses in sports cars, and making love in the ocean through the openings of expensive bathing suits!

She got into a taxi and fled back to her—or rather Nimr's— fancy apartment. She got out of the taxi and stepped onto the sidewalk opposite the apartment. Just as she started to cross the street, a sports car came roaring by and nearly ran her over. She herself escaped harm, but a little boy who had been crossing the street at the same time was hit by the car and thrown some distance through the air. She took off running and didn't stop to see what had happened to him.

She couldn't bear to go to the child to see what had become of him. His body wasn't moving, and he wasn't making a sound. Instead of going to his aid, she found herself collapsing on the pavement in tears. What a cruel city this was, including the people who lived there and especially its drivers!

She thought, that's exactly what happened to me, too: Nimr ran over me and didn't even bother to stop. And now I have to fend for myself.

Now she would have to decide whether to move to Nishan's apartment or to her brother's. She would have to choose once and for all between being a failed lover or a successful whore. As she wrestled with the decision that lay before her, she closed her eyes, trying to discern her real inner voice.

TWENTY-TWO

Yasmeena went back to her brother's apartment. Her purse was empty, since Nimr had stopped showering her with money several weeks earlier as part of his plan to get rid of her and shunt her onto someone else, and she was too shy to ask Nishan for money.

She had been in the throes of such torment throughout the previous few weeks that she'd forgotten about her brother. Not that she would have had any money to share with him anyway.

As she opened the door to the rather shabby apartment, she didn't feel distressed when she saw the worn-out wicker chairs, the walls without wallpaper or velvet, and the tile floor not covered by Persian rugs or shag carpets that one's bare feet sink down into. She only felt sad over leaving Nimr. It was a genuine grief unsurpassed by anything else she'd ever known, a grief as transparent and expansive as the desert sky, not like the pain of an addict who's been denied his fix, but rather like the suffering of someone who has been betrayed by the whole world even though he had given of himself in utter sincerity.

For the first time she was conscious of what it meant to be without Nimr. For her it was simple: she had bared to the sun her inner being, which had been brimming with love, and she'd given and given. She had continued to give despite her awareness that there were many other things that held sway over relationships in this city. Even so, she had never believed that Nimr would leave her. They had been joined into one flesh, even if only in a single moment of truthfulness. They had fused. And she had thought this was enough to bind them together forever! Even in her final miserable days with him, she hadn't believed that they would part. She'd had a vague sense of the approaching separation, like the awareness that a hunted animal has of the rifle of a hunter hiding in the bushes. But now, for the first time, she felt the bullet lodging in her heart, or rather, in her brain. For there had now appeared, beyond the translucent, all-encompassing fog of her grief, the shadowy specters of questions which had never before crossed her mind. She wondered to herself, if I'd known another man before Nimr—if they had allowed my body to experience wholesome, sound relationships in Damascus—would I have lost my way to this extent?

But what was the use of questions now that she was in such agony? Grief twined itself about her senses with octopus-like arms from which there was no escape.

How alone she was! If only her brother would come home! He was the one friend she could really count on. She should have realized this long before, but . . .

She was overjoyed when her brother came in. He, for his part, was surprised by her visit, and the moment he saw her, his face filled with rage. She remembered that she hadn't paid him anything for weeks. She hadn't paid what she owed him for remaining silent while his precious honor was being compromised. He shouted at her, "Well, it's good you finally showed up! I don't have a single piaster for tonight's party."

"Neither do I."

"How's that? And Nimr Bey Sakeeni?"

"He's getting married."

"You despicable liar! So then, you've started working on your own and you've got more than one lover now?"

He lunged at her and grabbed her handbag. Finding nothing in it, he flew into a rage. He began striking her repeatedly on the face, the blows coming in rapid succession along with his curses and insults.

"Where's the money, you slut?" he demanded. "Where? Where?"

Her face began bleeding profusely, and like a tigress, she found herself returning the blows without thinking. When her hand fell on his face, he went nearly insane with rage.

"So, you filthy whore," he screamed, "you hit back, too, eh? I'll slit your throat! I'll slit your throat!"

She wanted to say to him, "I'll pay you tomorrow—there's no need to start pretending all of a sudden that you're interested in defending your lofty honor!"

But her mouth was full of blood, and before she could say a word, the knife sank into her chest. She didn't feel anything but astonishment.

Half an hour later, her brother entered the nearest police station carrying a pail covered with a newspaper. He sat down in front of the officer on duty, removed the newspaper from the pail, and took out his sister's severed head, which was still dripping with blood.

In a manly voice he said, "I killed my sister in defense of my honor, and I want to make a complete confession."

A look of admiration flashed in the officer's eyes, but he returned the head to the pail and covered it up again fearfully. The brother then began making his confession while the clerk wrote it down, in his eyes, also, a look of appreciation and respect.

The officer sat for a while listening to the confession, but when he heard the name "Nimr," son of their region's parliamentary representative, he got up and went into the next room to make a telephone call. A few moments later, he was speaking on the phone in a hushed voice. "Abu Nimr Bey," he said, "sorry to bother you, but this is urgent!"

He began recounting some of what was happening, then ended the conversation by saying, "Of course, of course. I'll hold onto the record. No, I won't leak it to the newspapers or to anyone else. And I won't write up my report until you and your son get here. Whatever you say, sir, whatever you say, Faris Bey. At your service!"

TWENTY-THREE

Two slaps on the face.

"I am Nimr Faris Sakeeni, you dog! How dare you claim that I sullied your honor!"

"..."

"You should consider it an honor that I, the son of Faris Sakeeni, made love to your sister."

"..."

"The first police report has been destroyed, and now they're going to interrogate you again. You'll repeat what you said earlier about how you killed her for the sake of your honor. However, you will forget my name completely."

"..."

"You'll say that she had relations with numerous men. You won't mention my name, but instead you'll accuse her of practicing prostitution with a number of strangers. You'll forget my name completely."

"..."

"The autopsy will confirm that she wasn't a virgin, and I'll hire the best lawyers in the country to defend you. You'll be sentenced to only a few months, and during that time you'll forget my name. You won't forget it just in court but inside the prison as well."

"..."

"You won't go blabbing!"

"..."

"From this moment forward I'll consider you my employee. Beginning today, you'll be paid a monthly salary which you'll continue to receive throughout your prison term. Then when you're released you'll join my men, since we're always in need of people who are skilled in the use of a knife."

"..."

"If you don't do as I say, you won't even have the chance to appear in court. A fight will break out among the prisoners, and you'll be killed by accident in the melee. You won't live to ruin my reputation. And now, the choice is yours."

"..."

Two more slaps.

"Have you decided?"

Two more slaps.

"Have you decided?"

"I'm at your service, Bey. I've decided, I've decided . . . I've forgotten your name."

Then Yasmeena's brother collapsed in tears.

Killed by brother

Beirut as a character

Twenty-four

I just woke up.

Sleeping pills don't work anymore! I'm in constant torment, and I feel as though there are two men fighting inside my body.

When Nishan came to take me to the party, he got really angry. He shouted at me, "Farah, look at yourself in the mirror!"

He told me I was wearing women's clothing and that I had makeup on my face. I hadn't exactly noticed, but in any case, I don't know why it made him mad. He brought a doctor who stuck a needle into one of my veins. But I only pretended to go to sleep. They were talking about me, and Nishan was concerned about what he called my "crazy behavior." Anyway, I was pleased to hear him sounding so worried about me.

But I didn't sleep. I spent the whole night killing the ants that were coming out of my pillow to devour me.

And now that painful event has come back to me. It isn't a dream as they claim that it is. It really happens to me. I'll be walking along on stony ground, then suddenly it turns into loose sand under my feet, and little by little I'm swallowed up by the shifting sands. There's nothing anywhere around me but open, empty space—and a street sign with the name "Beirut" written on it. And I scream and scream and scream!

I've just woken up.

As usual, there are pictures of me in most of the newspapers. Farah, the "singer of manliness." What a joke! I've begun to find it difficult to read and I can't concentrate. Besides that, most things reported about me in the newspapers never happened to me. The fact is, nothing ever happens to me, even though the newspapers like to talk about all my love affairs! Maybe stories like that have been engineered by Nishan. Or maybe they really do happen to me and then I forget! I've become quite forgetful, and rather than reading anything, I content myself with looking at the pictures—most of all my own.

Here, lying in a pool of blood, is a slain woman whose head has been cut off. And here's a picture of the poor double-crossed woman before she died. I've seen this face before—but where, where? With Nishan in some restaurant? No, maybe they just look alike! But this one is thinner and younger. In the taxi. Yes, that's it. I saw her in the taxi on the way to Beirut. Now I remember it well. A funny thought occurred to me that day: for me to propose to her and for us to go right back to Damascus, get married, and forget about Beirut.

That's right. Once upon a time we met in a taxi. But it's no use trying to read the article. The words jump around under my eyes like fleas. The headline reads, "A Girl Murdered . . ." Ah! She gave me her address that day. I'll go out and march in her funeral procession. But where's that address? Where is it?

What's happening to me? Let me get up and put on my dress and my silk underwear. And let me try on that bra . . . I just adore those partly see-through lace brassieres. Then I'll go out looking for her funeral, or any other funeral. They're all the same, anyway.

What?

TWENTY-FIVE

The atmosphere of the clinic seemed like what one might find in the cabin of a spaceship.

"Nishan, you look distraught!" said the doctor. "What's happened?"

"It's Farah, Doctor. I don't know what's come over him! Sometimes he acts in the most peculiar way. He puts on women's clothes and wears makeup! And lately he's taken up a bizarre hobby: he goes around marching in any funeral procession that comes his way, without even knowing the person who died or anything else about it! He also has conversations with things that can't talk back—with the fish on his plate, for example, or with a roast chicken! I'm worried, really worried! His next concert is in twenty days, and I've already rented the theater where it's to be held. We've been advertising for more than a month now, and the tickets are all sold out. I've bet a lot on this guy—I've staked my reputation on him. What am I going to do?"

"Don't worry about a thing! Medicine can do miracles. Emotions are nothing but chemical reactions, and for every one of them there's a drug. . . ."

"He cries sometimes and says his spirit is broken!"

"There's no such thing as a 'spirit.' There are only chemical reactions, and I'll give him medicines that will guarantee the desired result. Human beings are mere clay in the hands of science, the master potter! Put your trust in modern medicine!"

"A Nightmare"

I looked everywhere, but it was no use!

I couldn't find the address of the girl who'd been murdered, the one who'd been my travel companion on the day I came to Beirut. I had to march in her funeral procession. As long as I'd thought of marrying her, even if only for a second, I considered myself a widower somehow. (Is there really a funeral for her, or is she in the autopsy room? No—they're having a funeral for her, and it should be large and elaborate.)

I went out into the streets looking for her, and oddly enough, I found her quite quickly! The procession was being led by some people playing horns, and behind them walked a group of Boy Scouts and other children. Her body was in a slow-moving black car festooned with wreaths and garlands, and behind it there was a large throng of people escorting her to her final resting place. I walked along with them, weeping and beating my breast. Then one of them asked me, "Are you the son of the deceased, the great man who lived abroad?"

I nearly hit him. This was *her* funeral—the funeral of the woman who had been my wife for a few moments in a dream. Then suddenly the funeral music turned into a wild jazz number. A hand emerged from inside the coffin and began throwing the flowers off of it. Then the lid of the coffin was removed and there she was—my "twin" on the journey to Beirut. Overflowing with vibrance and energy, she stood up inside the coffin (and she was so beautiful, God bless her!) and began to dance. However, none of them noticed, because they were all dead. She removed her clothes, one piece after another like a striptease dancer, and threw them onto the heads of the people walking in the funeral procession. But I was the only one who paid any attention to her. (Their heads were bowed, and they were all blue in the face, a caravan of the dead. But as she danced in her coffin, she seemed more lively than the waves of the sea. As for me, I was sure that once they arrived at the cemetery, they would all climb down into holes that had been dug for them before the stench of their rotting corpses began to spread.)

I thought to myself, we'll run away together, the two of us. And I burst out laughing at the foolishness of these dead people, who imagined themselves to be escorting a dead woman to her grave, yet they were more dead than she was! Let them look at how she dances with all the gaiety and merriment of which a body is capable. And I began laughing and laughing and laughing, and clapping to the rhythm of her dance.

Then someone hit me, and I was thrown out of the funeral procession and onto the sidewalk. Meanwhile, she disappeared, and the coffin remained open and empty.

"A Nightmare"

I decided that I needed a girl who loved me and whom I could love, someone who would pour laughter onto my desolate, lonely walls and wash my house and my eyes with sweetness and delicacy.

One day when Fifi and I ran into each other at the equestrian club, she said to me, "Hello. What's your sign?"

I replied, "I don't know my sign, but I know my name. . . ."

She was young and pretty in spite of her jangly, dissonant voice. She said, "Your name doesn't interest me. The important thing is your sign. I need to know if it fits me, if our signs will permit a relationship to develop between us!"

And she continued to chew her Chiclets with extraordinary enthusiasm.

I told her the first lie that came to mind. "My sign is Pisces." And she agreed immediately to go with me to my apartment, because Pisces was her favorite sign. In fact, she couldn't resist Pisces men. She also didn't like to waste time. As for me, though, I needed to catch my breath. So I convinced her that I had to pass by Wimpy's to get out of a previous engagement I'd made to meet someone there.

I rode with her in her sports car, which had a high-pitched, frightful, ferocious-sounding engine. In fact, the sound of it was like a cloud of violence, hatred, and fine black dust. (I'm falling into the cloud. I'm about to suffocate!)

She said that the sound of the engine excited her, aroused her desires. Then she took hold of my hand and slipped it between her knees. (There are copper containers shattering over my head. This wild din—augh! I'm dying to stretch out in a field of lettuce on the bosom of a woman so sweet and bashful that she trembles and shudders! Oh, for some gentleness, some tenderness!)

She then played a tape recording of the sound of her car taking off and the madness of its engines, and she turned the volume up full blast. As she laughed, her teeth looked like those of a vampire. I was afraid. I panicked and began to cry. Then all of a sudden she stopped the car and looked over at me inquisitively.

"So," she asked, "do you get high like me when the motor is racing? Ah! We'll make a fantastic couple! I love you! By the way, what's your name?"

We went into a cafe where Fifi ordered a Bloody Mary which she downed in a single gulp. After she'd emptied her glass, that cruel, devilish look came back into her eyes and into her kinky red hair. Then she picked up her straw, but instead of putting it into the glass, she inserted it matter-of-factly into my vein and began sucking my blood. She kept sucking and sucking until I began feeling dizzy.

I shouted at her, "Take this straw out of my vein, you vampire!"

Pretending to be upset, she gave me a look of shock and bewilderment, like someone who's found a crayfish in his morning glass of milk.

I began cursing and insulting her, saying, "Do you think you can deceive me, you whore? All you want is to suck my blood! I'll buy you liters of it from the blood bank, but leave me alone!"

Then I fled from her, and I could hear people whispering, "He's mad . . . mad . . ."

I grieved for them, because they were the ones who were mad, and blind as well. They simply hadn't noticed that their sweethearts were inserting straws into their veins to drink their blood. I shouted at them in an attempt to warn them, but they all just laughed.

People in this city certainly are strange!

The waiters at the first cafe threw me out, so I kept making the rounds to other cafes, but no one paid any attention to me. However, someone did look at me and say, "Isn't that the new star named Farah?"

The young woman accompanying him replied, "Impossible. But he does look a bit like him!"

"A Nightmare"

There are no longer two men fighting inside me. One of them has died, and that's that.

So now there is a dead man that I carry around inside me. He isn't completely dead, though, since now and then he wakes up and we cry together.

There's something mysterious about funerals that draws me to them. I don't know why I search them out and march in them.

Today I witnessed an amazing one. The coffin was covered with a white cloth. The mourners, also, were dressed in white and they were dancing. Everything glittered beneath the rays of the sun, and even the voices and sounds seemed to be white. I took off all my clothes to join in the amazing dance. But they beat me for stripping like that and told me I was crazy! (I was born naked, I'll be buried naked, and I like to go around naked as a jaybird!) Nishan came to the police station to get me released, but by the time I came out, the sun had disappeared.

It's exciting, the world of funerals! No two are alike.

But even so, all of them are similar in one way or another. They're all bound together by a single, transparent thread. Nevertheless, the thread is close to us, very close, as close as the noose is to the neck around which it's been wrapped.

"A Nightmare"

I now have a friend to talk to.

I bought her a bridal veil and a tiara of synthetic diamonds. After she'd put on the tiara, I placed the veil over it, and she looked beautiful and captivating.

When Nishan saw it, he asked me in alarm, "Where did you get this skull? And why are you putting a bride's crown and veil on it?"

He tried to throw it off the balcony, but I promised him that I'd do it myself. So I rescued her from him, ignoring his rebuke for my "crazy" behavior which was going to destroy "my future."

"A Nightmare"

Nishan decided that I should go to a toupee shop to pick out a suitable hairpiece for my new film, so I went escorted by the film director's assistant (or something like that).

I was calm and, as usual, complied with all of Nishan's orders so that I could become rich and famous like him. But then something strange happened that no one noticed but me.

In the toupee shop, the sales attendant brought me a collection of severed human heads that were still dripping with blood and said to me, "Pick out the hair that you like the most! One head costs fifty Lebanese pounds."

Their faces were covered with tears, and their lips were moving, though no sound was coming out. They obviously wanted to say something.

My escort then said to me, "Try this one."

He picked up a severed head, and to our surprise we discovered that it was hollow inside. He placed it over my head, and drops of cold, half-coagulated blood began flowing down onto my face.

I screamed and took off running. The owner of the shop grabbed me and said, "If you don't like this one, we'll bring you the one you request. Give us the specifications of the head you'd like, and we'll bring it to you. In fact, you can specify any head that strikes your fancy along the road, and we'll get it for you. Each one has a price, of course, but with us, nothing is out of the question."

Then the shop owner drew out a long knife with a thin blade that glinted in the sunlight, ready to bring me the head of any passerby whose hair I happened to like and wanted to have made into a toupee for myself.

And I fled.

"A NIGHTMARE"

Nishan and the film producer were in a restaurant together. They wanted to set a price for me and were discussing how much I was "worth."

On the wall I read a plaque that said in English, "The fish you eat today was swimming around yesterday."

I asked Nishan what it meant. Irritated, he replied, "It means your fish is fresh."

Then he returned to his conversation: "Only fifty thousand Lebanese pounds? You've got to be kidding! He made record sales in the month of . . . He's the star of the future!"

They brought a fish and placed it in front of me. I felt depressed as I thought about how just the day before it had been swimming around alive, and how every bite we take requires that some sort of crime be committed. The fish wriggled on the plate underneath the lemon and parsley. Then it jumped up laughing, gazing at me with its wide-open, lashless eyes.

"Are you really going to eat me?" it asked.

"I don't know!"

"But I'm still alive!"

"I don't know!"

"I'm also happy and want to live. How about you?"

"I don't know!"

"Pick me up and take me back to the sea. Would you?"

"I don't know!"

"Why are you so sad, like a fish that's been cooked in a filthy oven?"

"I don't know!"

"What are you doing here?"

"I don't know!"

"You look like a dead fish. Why don't *you* lie down here on this plate instead of me?"

"I don't know!"

"They'll stuff your mouth and ears with parsley, then draw it out through your nose. They'll cover you with lemon slices and lay you out on a big silver platter, then Nishan will serve you up at a big banquet. Is that really what you want?"

"I don't know!'

"Are you going to throw me back into the sea?"

"I don't know!"

"A Nightmare"

The driver stopped in front of the police checkpoint. The policeman said, "Passes! Identification cards! Passports!"

Then I was approached by a huge dog. It began sniffing me and making a terrifying, snorting sound. It made me think of the hyenas in the stories my mother used to tell me. My mother . . . what did I have to do anymore with my mother, my village, or anything else in my past? I felt like a different person, someone who didn't know me. I no longer knew myself.

"Your passes!" the policeman repeated gruffly.

The dog howled, and I was enveloped in a cloud of clamorous noise and violent scuffling. I got out my pass and stared at it. The picture on it was of someone laughing. But it wasn't my face! Farah? That wasn't my name! This piece of paper had nothing to do with me.

So I tore it up.

They didn't understand. They took me to the police station, and the next morning Nishan got me out.

"A Nightmare"

I woke up and found myself trapped inside a glass jar. Its walls were clear, but I couldn't pass through them.

Nishan picked me up in the jar and put me in his pocket, and I was about to suffocate. He took me to the warehouse of some apparel shop where they were shooting a film. When we arrived, he took me out of his pocket and put me down on a lovely leather chair. Never in my entire life had I seen a clothing store the likes of this one. It was decorated like the interior of a mansion, with marble walls, posh furniture, and lush carpet. And the mirrors, and the lights . . . But everyone there, like me, was a prisoner inside a jar, and no one could either hear or touch anyone else. Even so, everyone was talking at the same time.

The actress, who was beautiful and only half-clad, was hitting the walls of the jar that enclosed her. She was beating on them with both fists and screaming. . . .

The director slapped her.

I closed my eyes and wept secretly inside my jar.

(I can't bear to see tenderness in this world die!)

Had hours gone by? I don't know!

Nishan said to me, "I wanted to give you an inside view of the work, so you'd be aware of what's going on when you stand in front of the camera for the first time."

The filming stopped.

However, the brutal, remorseless stage lights remained directly on my face and on the area around me, while the surrounding shadows appeared grim, harsh, and inhuman.

Then most of the workers left the place.

Glasses of champagne were passed around, making little clinking sounds. . . . I drank a lot, quite a lot.

Then we were all transformed into a huge pile of naked flesh. We became an infernal octopus out of which emerged naked arms and legs, sighs, and moans as we rolled around on top of hot camera lenses and steel instruments with edges as sharp as knives.

Nishan's face was pressed against mine. I opened my eyes and stared at him. He had one eye in the center of his face, like a ghoul straight out of legends and myths. All of us were now inside a single, huge jar, like a can of rotten, putrefying sardines.

I struggled to get out, shouting, "This is Sodom and Gomorrah, only bottled inside a jar!"

"A Nightmare"

I opened my eyes. The walls were white and the furniture was beige. I was in a bed, and in front of me there was a woman wearing a nurse's uniform. A long rubber tube connected to a bag of serum came out of my arm, and a voice whispered, "A nervous breakdown . . ."

So then, I thought, I'm in the hospital. What happened? What are they doing to me?

I stared at the nurse. She wore a white cap, and she had the head of a wild boar. All the nurses had the heads of pigs or jackals. The doctor, who had an elephant's head, came and placed a stethoscope in his big ears.

Then I began to remember what had happened.

I'd been in a car and we'd run into something. When I opened my eyes, I was bleeding and crying and my body hurt all over.

There was a man shouting, "I can't let him in! There's no money in his pockets, and we don't know who he is. . . ."

Then I was approached by a face that asked me, "What's your name? What's your name?"

Thinking him to be the doctor, I tried to plead with him and beg him for mercy, but my voice wouldn't come out.

He whispered in my ear, "Do you have any money on you?"

" . . . "

"If I treat you, can you pay the fees?"

" . . . "

"If you don't have any money with you, I'll let you bleed to death. Like they say, 'If you've got a piaster, you're worth a piaster.'"

"..."

"Money, money! Do you understand?"

He took a large bill out of his pocket and poked my eyes out with it. Then I saw Nishan's face. . . .

The nurse approached, carrying a bag of serum with her hooves. When she got closer, I noticed that the bag of serum was actually a bottle of whiskey. She hung it up and the whiskey began to drip slowly into my blood. Laughing nonchalantly, everyone began dancing and singing while the doctor threw his scalpels into the air. Then they started playing catch with organs that had been surgically removed from various patients. I screamed and tried to take the whiskey serum I.V. out of my arm, but they tied me up with a man's intestines, wrapping them around me like ropes. They bound me so tightly I couldn't move, and an offensive odor filled the room.

Before I fainted, I saw a doctor making love to one of the nurses on top of the operating-room stretcher.

"A Nightmare"

In the public auction hall they had me stand up naked on top of a large table surrounded by middle-aged men and decrepit, senile old women. Their clothes, their jewelry, their diamond-studded spectacles, their long, gold-plated, ivory cigarette holders, and their silk gloves oozed with wealth.

"Groom for sale!" said Nishan. "A very lucky find! Who'd like a choice groom for his daughter? Which of you ladies would like to buy a groom like this, an authentic Syrian peasant, to keep her warm in her old age? He comes with youthfulness, a beautiful voice, and a future that's virtually assured!"

I wasn't completely naked. I was covering half of my face with a slave girl's veil studded with pearls, and from my waist there hung a gauzy blue silk scarf.

Nishan shouted happily, "Going once . . . going twice . . . sold!" The highest bid went to the late Ulwan Bey Al-Ulwan, who had lived abroad.

"Congratulations on the sale," Nishan whispered into my ear. "This marriage will be great publicity for you. Besides, it'll be good for your artistic career. Her father is rich and famous. So hang in there!"

"A Nightmare"

Supposedly, I was now a married man, and the woman next to me in bed was my wife, and I was supposed to . . .

I didn't feel any desire, but I grasped her arm. It was heavy. The room was pitch black, and I felt the arm come out of its socket. I threw it off the bed and took hold of the other one. It also came out of its socket, and I found myself holding nothing but a disconnected arm in my hand, so I threw it off the bed, too. Then I took hold of the head and pulled it toward me in a desperate attempt to possess my bride, but it came off, and nothing remained in my hands but a disconnected, bloodless head. I threw it onto the floor, and when it landed it made a hollow sound, like the falling of an empty container. Then I took hold of her leg, and it came off in my hands, so I threw it off the bed. When I took hold of the other leg, it came off, too.

Then I grabbed hold of what remained of the body and started looking for her breasts. I found them, but they had no nipples. And when I looked for her other female parts, I found nothing at all. At that point, I decided there was nothing else I could do, and I went to sleep. When I woke up at dawn, I found myself alone in the room, with bride parts still lying on the floor around the bed.

With the first rays of sunshine, I noticed that my bride was a mannequin like the ones in store windows—nothing but a mannequin. So why did Nishan get angry when I ran away?

"A Nightmare"

It was the night of my big singing concert. The seats, the walls, and the ceiling were all lined with people. The master of ceremonies gave me a fabulous introduction, and as I prepared to sing, I looked out over the crowd. Then, with all the grief and sorrow within me, all the confusion and all the lostness, I exploded.

I began to sing with all my heart, and the crowd began to laugh. I kept singing, and the crowd kept laughing.

The band left the stage, while Nishan beat his head with both hands. They said I'd howled like a wounded dog, that I hadn't sung a single word. All I did was howl and howl at the crowd.

I swore I'd been singing.

No one believed me. Instead, they took me to the hospital and said I was insane.

TWENTY-SIX

It's cold, cold. So cold, I'm chilled to the bone.

And this long winter will never end, never. . . . I've been crouching here in my hideout for I don't know how long. I know they'll look everywhere for me, and if they find me, they'll beat me.

They'll beat you, Farah, you pathetic creature. They'll dig their fangs right into your heart.

Yes, and I'll pant like a rabbit.

They'll put that white gown on me, tie my arms behind me, and take me back to the hospital like they did last time.

I'll weep and weep and weep.

They'll dump cold water on my head and tie me to the filthy bed in the bathroom-turned-torture-chamber. They'll enclose my head in a steel cap with wires coming out of it, then shoot electricity into my brain and forbid me to sing.

But no. They won't catch me this time.

I'll swear to them that I'm not crazy, that they're the ones who are crazy, and no one will believe me.

I'll swear to them that my nightmares are real, that they really happen to me, and to them, too. It's simply that they don't notice, since they're preoccupied with their own petty affairs and won't believe me.

It's cold, cold. So cold, I'm chilled to the bone.

I'll stay huddled here in my hideout until it gets dark, then I'll run away to my village. What's left of me is going back to Douma. I know that nothing will be like it was before, but still I'm going to run away, back into the arms of my Mother Earth. I've got to stay hidden without being afraid of my nightmares. I've got to be careful as I flee because Nishan is determined to get back at me with all the influence and money at his disposal.

He wants me in the insane asylum not to see me healed, but to take revenge on me, to torture me. He's the one who's ill, though, since he's the one who's able to accommodate himself to this sick society. As for me, I'm healthy. That's why I wasn't able to fall into a state of utter, absolute madness.

Ah—the day I came to Beirut, I was vaster than the night, and the sea itself wouldn't have been large enough for my bed. It seemed to me that the entire star-pierced canopy of darkness would be too small to contain my ambition and that all the women of Beirut wouldn't suffice me. All of its restaurants couldn't satisfy my hunger, nor could all its newspapers satisfy my pride. God, how broken I am, how scattered! And here I am now, gathering up the pieces of my broken self in a wretched hideout behind a garbage dump.

Beirut has withdrawn from me as the waves recede from the land, spitting me out onto the shore like a lonely, empty shell. I hear a voice sobbing inside me, like the sound of that shell. Oh, Beirut, how, how? . . .

"A Nightmare"

When I ran away from the hospital, the first thing I did was to steal the sign at the entrance that said "Hospital for the Mentally Ill."

I took it to the city entrance, removed the sign saying "Beirut," and planted the other one in its place.

I burst out laughing as I read the sign saying "Hospital for the Mentally Ill," with Beirut looming up behind it in dawn's light like an infernal wild beast preparing to pounce. And I ran away, fleeing to the safety of my lair. . . .

Author's Note

This work was begun on October 9, 1974. The first draft was completed by October 23, 1974, and all revisions were completed by November 22, 1974.

Class concepts- La Raza

- Bicultural
- imagined community
- counter hegemonic

Delgado Article- _____
- chicano national Identity in
  La Raza
  - Empowerment/cultural
                    affirmation
  - "It's in our blood to be an
                    Aztec warrior

     US vs. them - mentality
                   idea
★ 3 components of chicano national iden
- Empowerment/cultural affirmation

- call to Action

- Critique of institutional
                    authority
           - Delgado Bernal